WINTER WAR

Aftermath of Disaster Book 4

KEVIN BARRY MAGUIRE

KBM Publishing

ISBN: 978-1-950550-02-9

Kevin Barry Maguire
Visit my website at https://kevinbarrymaguire.com

Other books by Kevin Barry Maguire

In this series:

Aftermath of Disaster: Book 1 It Has Begun

Aftermath of Disaster: Book 2 Diggin' In

Aftermath of Disaster: Book 3 Summer's End

Aftermath of Disaster: Books 1, 2, and 3 Bundle

Non-Fiction

How to Get off the Grid and Survive

Prepper Journal & Inventory Logbook

Part I Josh and Sam

Josh

✿

JOSH MARTIN STROLLED THROUGH THE TACOMA Convention Center, admiring the weapons on display. He already made a few orders for his store in Puyallup. Now he was window shopping on his way out. He knows in about 15 minutes, the show floor will be closed for lunch, and locked down for an hour. Josh decided he didn't need to see anything else and left early for his store. Friday afternoon on Meridian Ave. is a nightmare, and he wanted to beat that traffic.

He jumped in his Bronco and set his package on the passenger seat. He made orders for his store, and they would deliver the weapons next week. The package contained a gift for himself - a Remington 1858 New Model Army .44 caliber handgun. It was a collector's item and would join all the others he bought to display at the store. He'll sell them if the price is right, but most people don't want to pay the price. *That's fine with me*, he thought. *I don't want to sell them, anyway.*

This one is a beauty - as far as one can be at this age. The barrel and cylinder had more than a few scratches and dings, but the wood handle was impeccable. It still bore the original handle, and the age was clear but beautiful. He couldn't imagine that grip had survived since the Civil War without so much as a ding. Josh knew the perfect spot to display this weapon - behind his register, high on the wall.

Meridian Ave. was busier than normal for early afternoon, but it wasn't a struggle yet. He cruised through a Wendy's drive-through for a quick sack lunch before arriving at his store. He grabbed his lunch and package and went inside.

"Hello Bruce, busy morning?"

"No sir, just one sale and four customers. Everyone must be at the gun show."

"No worries, we'll make up for it tomorrow. Go ahead and get some lunch, I got this."

Bruce stepped out from behind the counter and put on his jacket.

"And stop calling me 'sir,' it makes me feel old."

"Yes, sir."

Bruce left for lunch with a smile on his bearded face and Josh set the package down behind the counter. He'd get that on display later. His first order of business was to log his orders into the computer. As he was busy entering data, he got a message on his Apple watch:

#poisoned.

He knew he was to check Twitter for the hashtag and opened the app on his iPhone. He was reading posts from people all over the country complaining about being poisoned. As he was reading, he felt ill himself. He wrote it off as being a hypochondriac. Small beads of sweat formed on his forehead, and he felt nauseous. He kept telling himself he just imagined it.

Just as he was about to get back to his data entry, another hashtag buzzed his watch:

#radiationattack

That got his attention. He wiped his forehead and refreshed his Twitter feed and read the search results. In every major city in the country people felt the symptoms of radiation sickness. Nobody was sure who attacked or how, but everyone was certain it was radiation. Now Josh wasn't so certain he imagined his illness. He had been in Tacoma, after all. He knew Tacoma was a target of the attack.

As he was trying to decide whether to get to a hospital, the last message buzzed his watch:

SHTF.

He no longer needed to know what to do. The hospital would have to wait. His first order of business was to remove as many weapons as he could and get them to his safe-room at home. As Josh packed a few footlockers with weapons and ammo, Bruce walked in.

"Have you heard the news?" Josh asked.

"No boss, what's up?"

"We've been attacked. Radiation attacks across the country, Tacoma was hit. I was in Tacoma. I'm locking the store down and taking what I can. Grab what you can and keep yourself safe. If you have somewhere in the country to go, I suggest you go."

"Are you serious?"

"I'm not packing for my health."

Bruce looked around and grabbed an AK-47 then changed his mind and picked up an AR-15 instead.

Josh said, "Good choice. Those parts are easier to find. Take a few handguns too. You'll do good with a pair of night vision goggles and body armor. Don't be shy. If this turns out OK, you can bring them back. If not, use them well and save your ammo."

"I've got an Uncle in Humptulips, I'll get there and hunker down with him."

"Don't waste time getting there and you'll want to skip I-5. Get to Yelm on the back roads, then to Hwy 12. Get home and get your essentials, food, clothes, any other weapons you have. Think survival. And be quick about it."

"Yes, sir!" Bruce smiled and held his hand out to Josh. "It's been great working for you."

Josh took his hand and gave a hearty shake.

"You're a fine young man, Bruce. I hope to see you soon."

Bruce left with his gifts, and Josh continued packing. His main concerns were the AR-15's, night vision goggles, body armor, and ammo. In the spaces available, he added handguns and holsters. He didn't forget his precious rare handguns. Those will make good trade bait. By the time he finished, he had four footlockers filled. He slapped a lock on each one and loaded them into his Bronco. Then Josh locked the door and rolled the security door down and locked it. He did the same for the windows. It won't keep out everyone, but it will stop most people. *If I'm lucky, I'll get back to the store before that happens*, he thought.

Josh bought a house in Puyallup, near the store but out of the way. Behind his house is a grove of fir trees and behind them a "U-Cut" Christmas tree farm. It was as secluded as one could get without moving to the country. It only took him a few minutes to get there. He opened the gate and drove across the back lawn to the tree line. Hidden behind some bushes and camouflage was a door. He unlocked it and transferred the footlockers into the bunker. Then he threw up.

He was feeling worse now. A headache had developed, and the vomit didn't help. He got back in his Bronco and headed for Good Sam's Hospital. His friend was a doctor there. Getting there was difficult. He gave up driving a few blocks away and found a parking spot. By the time he got to the hospital, he felt weak and dizzy. Outside the front entrance was a triage area. He thought he saw his friend and dragged himself in that direction. Josh tried to scream "Sam!" but it was almost inaudible.

Then he heard his name, and someone sat him down.

Sam

❧

THE HOSPITAL HAD EXPERIENCED A DOWNTURN IN PATIENTS the past few months, but Dr. Sam Davis couldn't tell. He had more patients than he could handle and was still making rounds when he should have been at lunch. He'd grab a quick bite after he finished the rounds, then he had surgical consultation appointments scheduled. Tomorrow would bring more surgery and more patients to make rounds with.

"Good afternoon Mrs. Johanson," Sam said. "How is your new kidney treating you?" She smiled when she saw him, her lines showing she spent a lot of time smiling. He looked over her charts and the nurse's notes as she was talking. She was healthier than most women her age, healthy enough for a speedy recovery.

"Good afternoon, doctor. I'm OK today, I only have a little pain. I feel much better than yesterday."

"Well, that's good to hear. You're responding well, I think your body approves of its new organ."

As they were talking, Sam got a message on his watch but

didn't look. He wanted to give his patient his undivided attention.

"If things keep going this good, you can be home in a few days. Do you need anything?"

"A good IPA or a Mack & Jack's African Amber would go down nicely right about now." She was smiling but half serious. A girl could only drink so much water and juice.

Jack laughed and said, "Well, if you're going straight to alcohol, maybe we should keep you here another week." Jack winked and continued, "In all seriousness, you'll need to lay off the alcohol for a while still. Give your kidney time to acclimate before adding the extra duty of processing alcohol.

"Yes doctor, I understand. It's a good thing I didn't ask for some whiskey," she smiled again. "I always get a craving on a nice spring day. I'll wait it out, I like you, but I don't want to see you every day for the next week."

At that, they both laughed, and Sam said he'd check up on her again tomorrow. Then he glanced at his watch and saw the message. He still had one more patient to check on but put it off. He wanted to eat something and see what the message was about. Sam went to the cafeteria and bought a sandwich, coffee, and a bottle of water. As he found a table, his watch buzzed again, and Sam checked his phone. The first message was a moot point after seeing the second one about a radiation attack.

As Sam was reading, he couldn't believe his eyes. He saw Tacoma and Seattle got hit and knew they'd be getting patients soon. More than they could handle. He finished his sandwich as fast as he could and washed it down with the coffee. Then he called his wife.

"Marie, have you heard the news? Someone has attacked us."

"What? No. I haven't had a chance to turn on the TV. What's going on?"

He filled her in and said, "Call the kids and tell them you're coming for them. Get them home immediately."

"Yes, but what about you?"

"I'll be needed here," he said. "I may stay the night, it depends on the patient load. Once you're all home, get to the safe room. Nobody knows if there will be more attacks or how much radiation was released. One thing is for certain, it was a massive dose in the cities to affect people so fast."

"OK, call me when you know more, I love you."

"I love you too. Be safe."

Sam picked up his bottle of water and headed for the administration office. He needed to see if they knew what happened and make a plan for the influx of patients. He stepped into the office, and the secretary was already on the phone discussing patient load. So they knew what was going on. He waved to her and walked past her to the medical director.

"Bob, how are we handling this?" Sam said.

"We're still trying to determine the scope of the attack and how many people ambulances will bring here. The CDC will send potassium iodide, but we don't know how much or if we'll need it. We're also calling in the whole staff."

Sam said, "We'll need to set up a triage out front, I think. Everyone coming in will be contaminated. We'll need to decontaminate them, strip them, and wash them down before letting them in the hospital. So we'll need bins for the clothes, and a truck to dispose of the contaminated clothing."

Other nearby staff soon joined the two men, and they made their plan of action. Since Sam knew more about radiation treatment than the rest of the doctors, he would lead the triage team outside. It was no accident Sam knew so much, he is a prepper and has prepared for this situation.

The first order of business was to discharge anyone they could without danger to the person. Sam went through his patient's charts and released three of his surgical patients. Mrs. Johanson was happy to get out of the hospital early. When she heard about the attack, all she could think about was getting home to her cats. The other two patients were not so happy about leaving early.

While deciding which patients would go home, the maintenance staff was pulling beds out of storage and lining them in the hallways. Anywhere they could fit a bed had a bed, couch, or even a table for people to lie down. It made the hallways hard to navigate, but they weren't sure how many patients they would receive. They had to use every option to hold patients.

After they discharged patients and extra beds were made available, Sam spent his time working on the triage area. Everyone working outside in the triage area would wear full protective gear. The doctors and nurses wouldn't be in danger, as the victims were clean before reaching them. But Sam insisted it was better to be safe. He had maintenance bring large trash bins and stage them out front near the entrance driveway. Then they ran a hose to the area with a privacy screen. Everyone would disrobe and place their clothing in the bins. Then they would step behind the screen to get hosed down and scrubbed, then given a gown. When a clothing bin got full, a maintenance worker would pull the bag out, tie it up, and put it on a truck. Someone would drive the full truck to an incinerator.

Then they would proceed to the triage area, where Sam and a few other doctors would triage the patients. The most serious cases would get rooms while the less severe would get beds in the hallways. The first patients arrived before the staff finished the setup. When the first group showed up, Sam said, "Strip down to your underwear and place your clothing in one of the garbage bins. Place your personal belongings in a bag and carry it with you. The staff will sanitize your items while you're waiting for triage. Cell phones, keys, wallets, purses, etc. Wait in line in front of the privacy screen for a scrub down." It wasn't until they got behind the screen, they found out they would lose their underwear too. A few people objected and were told their clothes contained radiation and would continue to harm them, they reluctantly agreed. As the day wore on a few people still didn't want to remove their underwear. Their choices were to remove their underwear and get scrubbed or turn around and go home. With their clothing already mixed in garbage bins and some taken away, those people eventually agreed to the terms.

During a small break in the action, Sam called his wife to check on his family.

Sam said, "Hi hon, is everyone home safe?"

"Yes Sam, everyone is here and in the safe room. I'll stay here until at least tomorrow. By then we have more information."

"It looks like I'll be staying the night here. There is too much to do and too many patients for me to justify going home."

"Well, I hope you can come home at least for a little bit tomorrow so we can discuss things."

"If there is a way, I will be there. I need to get back to work, I love you."

"I love you too, honey."

The next group of victims came to the triage area, and everyone got back to work. They weren't seeing too many families because the children's hospitals were accepting adults so as not to break up families. While Sam was working on the patient, he looked up and thought he saw a friend of his. Then he heard a faint "Sam" and looked up again. Now he was sure it was his friend Josh.

"Hey! Orderlies! Get this man to the second floor, stat!"

Then Sam rushed over to his friend, who stumbled his way up to the triage area. Then he grabbed him and got him to the ground and asked his friend what the heck he was doing in Tacoma. He knew Josh carried and gave him a quick frisk. Being careful so nobody saw, Sam slid the holster and weapon from Josh's back and tucked it under him. Then he called a nurse for help.

"Nicole! Come help me get this man undressed!"

Sam and Nicole undressed Josh and escorted him to the shower. Sam wondered why his protective suit didn't have a pocket and turned away from the crowd and picked up the weapon. He told a fellow doctor he needed to take a minute and walked towards the parking garage. Sam removed his hood and pulled down his protective suit and stowed the weapon in the small of his back. Without wasting a second, he closed his suit and got back to the triage area so he could help Josh.

Nicole handed Sam a new pair of gloves and reminded him that his were contaminated. After seeing his friend in bad condition and worrying about the weapon, the gloves slipped his mind. He took two risks holding Josh's weapon. First, it was contaminated. Second, if someone caught him with it, he would lose his job. In normal times he would lose his job, but today is not normal.

When Josh came out of the shower, Sam grabbed him and looked him over.

Sam said, "Where were you at 12:30 today?"

"I was at a gun show at the Tacoma Convention Center." His voice was raspy, and he spoke slow.

"How long were you there? When did you leave?"

"I got there at about 8:30 but didn't stay all day. I left before 1:00, maybe 12:45?"

"Well, the good news is you weren't affected for long. The bad news is, to be this sick for 15 minutes of exposure means you were very close to the source. I think you will recover, however. I'll send you to my ward."

Sam waived a few staff members over and said, "Get this man to the third floor, surgical."

As Josh disappeared behind the doors, Sam heard a lot of vehicles coming up the drive and wondered if they can handle the victims that many vehicles would hold. When the vehicles came into view, however, he saw they were military. *Well, this can't be good*, he thought.

The convoy stopped in front of the triage area, and a man stepped out of the lead vehicle. Sam walked up to him and asked what was going on. The man looked to be in his mid-50's and average height. He looked to be in great shape for a man his age, or any age for that matter. Sam saw birds on the man's collar, and he carried himself with an air of authority.

The man said, "I'm Colonel Jefferson, and we're here to protect you. Who's in charge and where can I find them?"

"You can find Bob Nelson on the fifth floor. Follow the signs to the administration office. Who do we need protection from?"

"Thank you."

Without saying another word, the colonel marched into the hospital. A few of the vehicles went into the parking garage, and the rest took up positions around the hospital.

The Day After

THE ALARM ON SAM'S PHONE WENT OFF AT 7 AM. THE large couch in his office made a comfortable bed. He had spent many nights on that couch, so it was nothing new. He folded his blanket and sheet, picked up his pillow and put them all in his closet. He was the best surgeon in the hospital, and his office reflected that. It was a nice corner office with a view of the Puyallup Fairgrounds. His desk sat opposite the windows so he could see the fairgrounds. The couch was on his right when sitting and his closet on the left. A rocking chair sat under the window, and he had two comfortable chairs in front of his desk. He even had a small bathroom, but still had to use the staff showers when needed.

Sam got dressed in the same clothes he had on yesterday, except for his socks and underwear. He kept a few clean pairs in his closet. I'll need to get home and get some fresh clothes today, he thought. He usually had an extra shirt and t-shirt in the closet too. But he forgot to replace them after using them last week. *A fine prepper you make*, he thought. Sam grabbed his phone and headed for the café.

Once there, he got a large cup of coffee, bacon, eggs, and some hash browns. On a normal day, Sam would pick up a newspaper and read while he ate. But for the first time in forever, the printing presses missed a day and did not run. He looked around for an empty table and noticed the soldiers taking up a lot of space. He chose a table next to two soldiers hoping to pick up on their conversation.

He was able to get a little news on his phone, but none of the information was new. If the soldiers knew anything, they kept it to themselves. The only thing on their minds was getting home to their families and hoping they were safe. Sam still wondered why the hospital needed protection and who they needed protection from. He got a bad feeling when the colonel wouldn't answer the question.

After breakfast and his disappointing intelligence collection, Sam made his way back to his ward to check in on his patients. His first stop was his friend Josh. He stepped in the room and saw Josh was still asleep. He went over the charts to make sure nothing changed overnight. It didn't look like Josh suffered any internal damage and Sam expected him to make a full recovery. But Sam wasn't taking any chances with his friend. He made sure Josh received potassium iodide, Prussian blue, and DTPA. He was too close to the radiation source for comfort.

Josh stirred and opened his eyes. He looked up at Sam and gave a small smile, it was the best he could do in the situation. Sam smiled back at him and said, "Good morning, tough guy."

Josh shook his head, "Not tough, just lucky."

"So tell me what hurts this morning."

"Talking hurts right now. Can we talk later?"

"Of course we can. I'll be here all day, I think."

Sam poured a glass of water for Josh and set it on the table next to his bed. He gave a nod to his friend and went to check on the next patient.

❦

After Sam finished his rounds, he went to talk to Bob. The secretary motion form to sit down and Sam took a seat on the recliner.

Sam said, "How long do you expect he'll be busy?"

"He is speaking with the colonel right now. It's been about 10 minutes, so I don't expect it to be too much longer," the secretary said.

A few minutes later everyone in the area heard Bob's voice through the door and walls, "That is unacceptable! We have families too, we need to check on our families and know they're okay."

The colonel kept his voice low, so Sam wasn't able to hear the response. But about a minute later the colonel walked out of Bob's office and out into the hall. Sam looked at the secretary and she nodded, so he got up and walked into Bob's office.

"I couldn't help but overhear you were upset. I came here to see about going home and checking on my family and maybe get a change of clothes or two. I have a sinking feeling that isn't about to happen anytime soon."

"I'm sorry Sam. The colonel said the entire staff is needed here and it would be day-to-day whether we can get home for a break. I tried to reason with him, but he would have none of it."

Sam said, "My wife will not be happy to hear this. I expect my children won't be too happy either. I've got one pair of clean underwear and socks left, and I'm still wearing the same clothes as yesterday. After spending several hours in the protective gear, I was a little sweaty. So I know my shirt doesn't smell spring fresh."

"I can open the laundry service for the staff. You'll have to wear a gown while your clothes get cleaned. It's a small price to pay for smelling spring fresh," Bob said.

"That's a small consolation, but I'll take it. I won't be paying the price, however. I also keep a robe in my closet. Always be prepared."

"Well, you're more ahead of the game than the rest of us."

Sam got up to leave and remembered to ask the burning question, "Yesterday the colonel said they were here to protect us. Did he ever say who they were protecting us from?"

"I wish I had that answer for you, but the colonel only demands and doesn't give."

Sam shook his head and walked out the door.

When Sam left the office, he took out his phone and called his wife.

"Hi, honey. How are you and the kids?"

"We're doing good, everyone slept well considering the circumstances."

"My couch treated me well, and I suspect my breakfast was better than yours, but I have some bad news."

"I knew it. You aren't coming home today, are you?"

"I just came out of Bob's office and the Army officer 'protecting' us said nobody was going home until further notice. We don't know what that means or how long it will be."

"What do they expect you to do about your family?"

"I don't like it any more than you do," Sam said. "One hundred disaster scenarios run through my mind every hour, and it kills me that I'm not there with you. The soldiers are in the same boat as we are. They all have families too."

"Well not worried about them or their families, I'm worried about you and us."

"You can probably come out of the safe room now. Nothing new has happened. I will get home as soon as possible, you can count on that."

"Sorry, I'm upset but not at you. I know you will. I'll talk to you soon."

At that, they hung up and Sam went to consult with a few doctors.

❦

Monday morning Sam again went to see Josh first. He looked over the charts and saw nothing that alarmed him. Josh was still asleep, so Sam sat in the chair and waited for him to wake up. Sam thought about their times at the gun range and in the Bald Hills firing off rounds. Josh taught Sam almost everything he knows about guns and marksmanship. It was a little ironic that a surgeon dedicated to saving lives could take out a man at 400 yards with ease.

After a few minutes of reminiscing, Josh rolled over and

opened his eyes. Sam said, "Good morning. How was your sleep?"

"I only woke up a few times during the night. I feel a little better, or maybe it's wishful thinking. I hope I look better, but I can't see the mirror."

"Maybe you look a little better, or maybe I'm just trying to get rid of you."

Sam laughed, and Josh managed a smile. Sam reminisced, and the two men talked about better days, guns, and good times. Since Sam was stuck at the hospital all day and all night, he wasn't worried about spending a lot of time with Josh. There was plenty of time to get to his other patients. If anyone needed him, the nurses knew where he was. Sam spent about an hour with Josh and was excited to see improvement in his attitude and responsiveness.

While Sam was making his rounds, he got a call from his wife. He ignored it the first time because he was with a patient, but when she called back immediately, he knew he had to accept the call. He excused himself and walked out to the hallway.

"Hello hon, what's up?"

"Sam, you're not going to believe this! There is a military truck outside installing cameras on the polls and pointing them at our house."

"Are you kidding me? You're right, I can't believe this. What the heck is going on? First they tell us we can't leave and now this?"

"I don't like this one bit. Talk to whoever you need to talk to and get these cameras removed, or I will go all Annie Oakley on those cameras."

"Stay calm, I'll talk to Bob and see what's going on. Don't shoot the cameras, the last thing we need is you in jail and me stuck at the hospital."

"Fine. I won't shoot the cameras. But they better get removed."

"I'll see what I can do."

Sam finished his rounds and made his way to Bob's office and asked him if he knew about the cameras. Bob said he's already got a few complaints, and he's waiting for the colonel to give them some answers. Just then the colonel walked in and asked what he needed.

Bob said, "I've been getting complaints from the staff that military personnel are installing cameras outside the houses and pointing them at their homes. I think you are overstepping your authority and your soldiers must remove those cameras."

The colonel seemed unfazed by Bob's demand and said, "The cameras are there for protection. At this time doctors and nurses are in high demand, and we fear people may want to harm you. We're here to keep you safe, and the cameras are to keep the families safe. The staff here at the hospital won't have to worry about their families because we are protecting them. Besides the cameras, roving patrols are making sure the area is safe."

Sam interrupted and said, "You keep mentioning your protecting us, but you never say who you're protecting us from. So please enlighten me, who is this enemy that wants to harm doctors and nurses?"

The colonel replied, "You worry about healing people and I'll worry about protecting people. The less you know, the less you need to worry about and the more effective you will be."

Sam looked incredulous and said, "I'm not a five-year-old, and I don't need you protecting my psyche. You have us trapped in the hospital and now you're spying on our families. I want an explanation."

The colonel wasn't accustomed to people making demands of him and was unprepared to give an answer. In response to Sam's demand, he stood up and walked out the door.

Bob said, "Well that went swimmingly."

"I don't trust that man, Bob. He's holding too many secrets. I don't believe you're protecting us, I believe we're you are holding us prisoner."

❧

The next morning when Sam went to visit Josh on the morning rounds, he took the notebook with him. He needed to ask Josh for help and didn't trust the colonel didn't bug the rooms. Even if the soldiers didn't but the rooms, he didn't want anyone to overhear them. Sam already wrote in the notebook to save time.

I need you to stay behind after I have released you. The military isn't letting us leave, and I'd like you to watch over my family. Then when the time comes, help me escape.

Sam began a story and handed the notebook and a pen to Josh. He read the note and wrote a short reply:

You can count on me.

Sam nodded his head and tore the page from the notebook. Then he crumpled it up and threw it in the toilet. The two men talked for about an hour and just before Sam left, he flushed the toilet.

The Plan

TODAY MARKS TWO WEEKS SINCE THE ATTACK. ABOUT A week ago, cell phones stopped working, and the power went out across the country. Sam finally saw his family last week. Two soldiers escorted to and from his house via Humvee, for his safety of course. He slept in his own bed for one night and snuggled close to his wife. He was certain they were listening to him and his family and took no chances talking openly about his plan. Sam used his notebook to tell his wife that Josh would stay behind and help him escape. They only had to wait for Josh to recover.

The colonel wasn't free with any information. The best Sam could guess, from overhearing soldiers, the power grid got hacked and destroyed. Nobody was sure why cell phones stopped working but assumed it was another hack. The only good thing about the military being at the hospital was they had fuel. When surgery was necessary, they could fire up the generators. The military set up a canteen was fed everyone at the hospital. Some would consider that a good thing until they ate it. It kept them alive, however.

Sam talked the colonel into letting him go for a run every day. But two soldiers followed him in a Humvee, for his safety again. For the first time since he met the colonel, he believed him. Some sketchy characters were walking around, and Sam figured without his escort, he might have been in trouble. He developed a rough plan for his escape, and this route would be a part of the plan. He ran the same route every day to lull his guards. By seeing the same thing every day, their minds would shut out what was going on around them. He hadn't figured out the rest yet, but he was sure Josh and himself would come up with something.

Sam jumped off the couch and got dressed. His wife provided the clean clothes. She and the kids washed all their clothes the old-fashioned way, with a twist. They bought two off-grid washing machines powered by a hand crank. Sam's house had solar panels and batteries but not enough to power the washer and dryer. They used the power for communications and some cooking. He thought they'd be using it to keep their phones charged too, but those are worthless paper-weights now. Turning on the lights was a no-go. They didn't want neighbors knowing they had electricity.

She only drove to the hospital herself once, then gas became scarce, and they needed to save it for their escape. Now she used the cameras to her advantage. When she needed a soldier, she walked outside, faced the camera and waved her arms frantically. In quick order, a Humvee would arrive with two soldiers. Marie would then hand them a note to pass to her husband, or a bag with his clean clothes. Sam would trade bags given to soldiers with his dirty clothes to return home. He told the colonel it was the least they could do for keeping him prisoner.

Sam made his way to the mess tent outside, provided by the

military. He used to think he'd get information here by sitting close to soldiers and trying to hear the conversations. But the soldiers used good discipline in the tent and stuck to clean conversations. Sam never got any useful information here. For that, he had to take short walks outside and approached soldiers without being seen or heard. Using this method is how he found out the cell phone towers got hacked and released a virus to cell phones in the towers themselves.

He finished his breakfast of powdered scrambled eggs, indescribable meat, and watered-down coffee. He finished his morning routine by visiting Josh again.

Sam said, "Good morning sleepy head. It's good to see you waking up at a decent hour again."

"Hey, you try taking a heavy dose of radiation and see if you feel like climbing a mountain."

"I'm really impressed about your recovery. I want to release you next week or the week after. Most people are being sent to the fairgrounds because FEMA set up a large camp there. That's how the fairgrounds came into existence. Back in World War II, it was a Japanese internment camp. History repeats, sort of, anyway. I don't know if their prisoners are not. But you'll be offered the choice to go there."

Josh laughed, and Sam joined him. They both knew Josh would never step foot in that camp.

Sam said, "Don't worry, I'll vouch for you with the colonel and let them know you have somewhere to go outside the zone."

"That makes me happy."

Sam pulled out his notebook and handed it to Josh, the first message already written. He told a short story while Josh read the note and replied.

I have the beginning of the plan worked out. I'm running the same route every day for two reasons: 1. To lull the guards into a false sense of security; 2. So I could look for possible escape routes. I head up Meridian Street and turn right at Cascade Christian schools, onto an unnamed road that curves around the 21st Ave. then back to Meridian right, on 23rd Ave. SE. then left on 7th St., East to get back to the hospital. It's a big circle with a side trip. I told my escorts it was to add a little more distance to my route, and they bought it. The real reason for the little side trip? That is how we create my escape.

You need to find a box truck and wait for me. When you see me, start backing out slowly into the street to block the Humvee. You should place the truck in position first, and then drive the Bronco to the location. I will run around the truck and if we're lucky, the soldiers won't realize what's going on until we've had a head start. I'll need you to scout out where we go from there and where to pick up my family.

Josh thought for a moment and then wrote:

I'll work something out. I've got a lot of trade bait and I'm sure I can get a truck, especially for short-term. I'll meet with Marie and work out the details with her. I can fill you in by coming back for a checkup, and we can finalize the date and time.

Sam read the reply and nodded. As usual, he tore the page from the notebook and crumpled it up. Then he went to the toilet in the room and flushed it down. Sam talked with Josh for a little while longer then continued his rounds.

The day had finally come for Josh to go home. He hadn't fully recovered, far from it. But he was well enough to go home.

Josh said, "Thanks for the excellent care, friend. I'm lucky to have you and have you so near."

Sam replied, "Don't mention it, I was only doing my job. I did nothing for you I wouldn't have done for someone else."

Sam winked and smiled.

Sam handed Josh a notebook and a pen and said, "Here's a parting gift, use it wisely with good friends."

"I think I know of just such company." Now was Josh's turn to wink.

Sam handed Josh a bag and said, "The Red Cross has provided clothes for all the patients that lost theirs. I guessed your size so they may not fit well and they is no way they're gonna look good. But they are serviceable, and they will get you home."

"That's the best I can ask for under the circumstances. Now I have to hope my Bronco is still where I left it."

"You may get lucky with all the military vehicles running around. They are keeping the general vicinity safe. Go get dressed and walk with me to my office. I have one more thing for you."

Josh was curious but said nothing. He slipped off his gown and got into the close provided. Then they made their way to Sam's office and once inside, Sam shut the door and locked it. He placed a finger over his mouth with a silent "shush." Then he pulled out his keys and unlocked his closet. Sam reached beneath his bare bedding and pulled Josh's weapon and holster from underneath.

Josh's eyes lit up, he smiled and shook his head. He placed the holster in the small of his back and hooked it to his belt. He was glad Sam picked a nice belt for him.

Sam said, "Take one of these once a day to help keep the nausea away."

Sam gave Josh a prescription bottle with pills to control nausea. That gave him a reason to get Josh into his office to receive his weapon. If anyone was listening, this would be the excuse.

Sam said, "Take good care of yourself and go get some fresh air. I'll walk you out."

⁂

Josh found his Bronco in relatively good condition. There was a little spray paint added with colorful words and a tag he couldn't read. There were a few scratches on the driver side door around the lock and handle. Someone had attempted to unlock the truck, and either failed or something scared them away, and they didn't come back. He got in and drove home before visiting Sam's wife, Marie. Things were different when he arrived, like the broken window out front. He didn't expect to find too much of value left inside but wasn't too worried. Everything he needed to survive was locked up tight.

The first thing Josh did was grab a slab of plywood, nails, and a hammer. Then he got to work boarding up the window. When he finished that chore, he went into the basement and moved a few things around. Then he uncovered a keypad and punched in a combination. A door slid open revealing his safe room. The solar panels on the roof provided the electricity. Batteries were hidden elsewhere in the basement. He fired up his computer and sent a message to Paul Peterson:

Paul,

I hope this note finds you well.

I'm writing to let you know Sam and I are safe and in good condition. I got caught in the radiation and Sam just released me from the hospital. The National Guard is keeping the entire hospital staff prisoner. They say it's to keep them safe but we're not sure of their true intentions. Either way, we've developed a plan to get him out. No date set. But we should be at your location within 2 to 4 weeks.

With that finished, Josh locked up his safe room and left to visit Marie.

❧

Josh pulled into the driveway and got out of his Bronco. He looked around and noted the camera positions. Then he walked up to the door and rang the bell. Soon the door opened and a young girl with long brown hair popped out. She was around 13 years old and said, "Hi Josh, you look better than I thought you would. I was hoping to see some scars!"

"It's good to see you too, Viktoriya. I need to speak with your mother, is she around?"

"Yeah, she's outback doing laundry. I'll go get her, come in and have a seat."

The living room in this four-bedroom rambler was bigger than it looked from outside. There was a wood-burning stove in the corner, a couch and love seat, and a big comfortable recliner that Josh fell into. He reclined the chair and put his hands behind his head. He looked around at the useless TV and game systems. He ached to fire them up, but it was too risky. He would get too excited and attract outside attention.

About a minute after he sat down, a rather short woman with long blonde hair entered the room drying her hands with a towel.

Hello Josh, it's good to see you up and around. What brings you here?"

"Sam sent me to see how everyone was doing and if you needed anything. But listen, I spent too much time laying down in a bed. Do you mind if we take a walk and catch up?"

"That sounds like a great idea! Viktoriya and Kevin, finish the laundry while Josh and I take a walk! Let me grab a little protection and a jacket and will get going."

Marie went into her room put on her shoulder holster and stowed her 9mm. Then she put on a light jacket and walked back out to the living room. Josh was up and waiting and they walked out. Marie was sure to lock the door behind her. They made their way to Woodland Avenue and cut into the trees heading for Clark's Creek Park. No vehicles had followed them, however. When they got to the park, they kept walking just in case anyone was following them. It was harder to catch a moving target. Josh didn't think the house the military bugged the house but respected Sam and knew it was better safe than sorry.

Josh kept his voice low and explained the plan to free Sam from the hospital. He told her she would need to prepare to leave and get everything packed and ready to go. He would give her a few days warning so she can get the solar panels and batteries removed.

Then Josh said, "About those cameras, those could be a problem. Does anyone follow you when you drive away?"

She replied, "So far, a vehicle finds me each time. There is always at least one vehicle in the neighborhood."

"Okay, this is what I need you to do. Drive to a friend's house regularly and stay for at least an hour. Keep an eye on your escort and monitor their reaction."

"I can see one problem with that. That will take a lot of gas, and that is in short supply. My Blazer doesn't get the best mileage. We have spare gas, but we need to save that for when we get out of Dodge."

"No worries, drive by my place and I'll top you off. Choose a friend who lives close, preferably in the neighborhood because will need to get you to the meeting place on 5th St., SE.

"All right, I think I know just the person.

Prisoner

SAM MISSED TALKING TO HIS FRIEND EVERY MORNING. HE had to make do with his patients and fellow staff members. He got along with the other doctors and nurses and even liked a few, but he wouldn't consider any of them his friend. Sam had discharged most of his radiation patients. But the FEMA camp across the highway sent a steady stream of new patients. From the stories the patients told, the camp was no summer picnic. Some of the patient's troubles included stabbings, STDs, assault, and even rape. The STDs were coming from prostitution running wild inside the camp. Women and men are turning to prostitution to feed themselves and/or their families.

Sam was making his morning rounds, and his next patient was a young lady who picked up chlamydia in the camp. This was not Sam's area of expertise, but with beds filled everywhere, people ended up wherever a bed was available. He knew who to consult if he had questions.

Sam said, "Miss. Roberts?"

The young woman replied, "Mrs. Roberts." She was dirty and didn't look like she'd had a shower in a week or two. Her shoulder length red hair was greasy and uncombed. Her clothes needed a good washing too. Under all the dirt, Sam thought she might be in her upper 20s or low 30s.

"I'm sorry, Mrs. Roberts. I've seen a lot of patients come and go and I just assumed. Before I assume again, did you pick the chlamydia up in the camp?"

"Yes, and to answer your next question, I was trading favors for food to feed my boy." She looked at the floor as she said the last part.

"I'm not here to judge you, only to help. FEMA isn't feeding you there?"

"We get fed twice a day, half rations. It's not enough for my baby. Money is worthless there. There are only two ways to get what you want, food and favors. We need the food so... You may not believe me, but before all this happened I was an accountant working at the casino in fife. We had a good life. Now we struggle to survive. We thought the FEMA camp was the best choice, but I think we would've been better off almost anywhere else."

"I don't know how to improve your life at the camp, but I can give you a start by cleaning you up. I'll have the nurse here take you to the showers so you can wash away that dirt and grime. Then I'll get you some new clothes. Does FEMA provide condoms?"

"No. All we really get from them is a bed and a little bit of food."

"When you come back, I'll have some antibiotics for you and your husband, just in case. You need to refrain from 'favors' for the next seven days. It should be cleared up by then."

Mrs. Roberts felt overwhelmed, and tears welled up in her amber eyes. She looked Sam in the eyes and said, "Thank you, I don't know what to say. I forgot there was a time when people did things without expecting something in return."

"Don't mention it." Sam looked at the nurse and said, "Nicole, can you escort this young lady to the showers and pick up some nice clothes for her?"

"It would be my pleasure, doctor."

৩৯৩

Sam finished his rounds and went to see Bob again. Ever since he spoke with Mrs. Roberts, it nagged at him that the people at the FEMA camp weren't properly cared for. For the first time since the military took over the hospital, he felt a spark of gratitude. Even though he was effectively a prisoner, he had it much better than others. That did not forgive taking his freedom, however. When he got to the office, the secretary motioned for him to have a seat. She said, "the colonel is in there, I don't know how long he will be."

Sam waited for about five minutes, and the door finally opened. The colonel saw Sam getting up and walked over to him.

He raised his hand to shake Sam's and said, "You're the doctor who runs every day, correct?"

Sam stalled on the handshake then raised his arm in a slow and easy manner. "Yes, I run daily."

"If you don't mind, I'd like to run with you."

Sam took a deep breath and replied, "Maybe you should run with someone in your age bracket."

"I like to run with the younger guys, it ensures I stay in good shape."

Sam didn't like this idea at all, of course. The last thing he needed was the man in charge running next to him when he was trying to escape. That would add a new dimension to the plan and significantly lower the chance of success.

Sam took another deep breath and said, "You have given me no answers since the day you arrived. I don't like a man who keeps secrets. Until you can treat me with respect and answer my questions, we are not running buddies and we are certainly not friends."

The colonel jerked his head back and his body stiffened, but he didn't say a word. He turned and walked out of the office. Sam walked through the open door and sat down in front of Bob's desk. Bob shook his head but had a smile on his face. He told Sam, "I don't think you should've talked to him like that, but I'm glad you did. Someone had to jerk that stick out of his butt."

"Well I there is no way I want to run with him, and he wasn't taking the hint. I was pretty sure he still would not give me the answers I wanted, so it was a great way to get rid of him. I came here to see if we could help the FEMA camp at the Puyallup Fairgrounds. We're getting an abundance of patients with STDs, and I found out FEMA doesn't hand out condoms. I know we've got a bunch, and I thought we can donate a majority to the camp. It would do wonders in freeing up our time."

"I'll have someone box them up and see if I can get the

colonel to get them delivered. Assuming he's recovered from your little outburst."

The two men had a good laugh, and Sam left to get in his run for the day.

❁

Sam changed into his running gear and walked out the front of the hospital to meet his escort. He saw the two guards and a third man was with them, wearing a T-shirt and shorts with sneakers. Sam recognized the colonel and dread filled his heart. When he dressed the colonel down, it wasn't to get information. It was to keep the man away from his escape route. The information would be welcome, however. Sam walked up to the group and told the guards he was ready. He said nothing to the colonel.

Sam started running and made his way to Meridian Avenue. He hoped the colonel would run elsewhere, but that hope was soon lost as the old man ran up beside him.

"Doctor... I'm sorry I don't know your name."

Sam gave in and said, "Davis."

"I'm Colonel Jefferson with the Washington National Guard. I know you have questions because I've heard you ask them. There isn't a whole lot I can say except we are here to protect the hospital and its staff. I didn't lie when I said that before. In the beginning, we thought it was just the radiation and things would get back to normal soon enough. But then we lost cell phones and electricity. I'm not sure there will be a normal again, but that's between you and me. You doctors and nurses are a valuable resource, and we can't let anything bad happen to you. If we weren't here, the derelicts would overrun you trying to get to your drugs."

Sam listened intently, and it surprised him the colonel was saying so much. So he didn't answer, hoping he would give up much more.

The colonel continued, "Before the bad actors could take advantage of the situation, we secured every pharmacy we could. Those we couldn't, we contacted the local police force and put them to the task. We eventually cleared all the pharmacies of the medications, and we have them warehoused throughout the state. Bob knows to contact me with anything he needs. You don't know this but thieves shot a few of my men, and a few were killed securing those pharmacies. I'm certain if we weren't protecting the hospitals, most of you would be dead already. We've gone out of our way to make sure your families are protected as well. If your wife needs anything, she only needs to ask."

Sam digested this influx of information and stayed quiet for a few more minutes. Then he said, "I'm sorry for the silence. That was a lot of information and I had to think it through. I'm not ungrateful and I know many people have it much worse. I see it in the patients from the FEMA camp. They have it terrible and are in need of more help. However, I do not appreciate being held prisoner and being told when I can see my family, or when I can leave the hospital. My family and I have prepared for just about every situation, and I can assure you I would not be among the dead had you not arrived. I would've taken my family to a safe location we had prepared a long time ago. I would eat better on my own, for sure. Those things you call eggs should be banned."

Colonel Jefferson laughed and said, "You get used to them after five or ten years."

The two men continued to chat as they ran and Sam even felt himself liking the guy. But he also thought about how to get rid of him when it was time to escape.

❧

Sam took a shower after the run and went back to his office. Josh was waiting for him and Sam lit up when they shook hands. Sam said, "It's good to see you again, you're looking much better. Step inside my office and I'll give you a checkup."

"It's good to see you too, doctor."

They went inside and Sam did give his friend a checkup before getting into personal matters. There was no sense in wasting the trip and it needed to get done. Sam said, "Everything looks good so far. I see nothing out of the ordinary at this time."

"Great, I have a hot date with a glowing brunette later on."

Josh raised his eyebrows a few times and smiled. He handed Sam a notebook and told a story about his favorite brunette while Sam read.

I found our escape route. We will cut through some yards on a sparsely populated block and eventually get to 7th St E. We'll pick your family up further down the road. Should anything go wrong, and I expect it might, we'll head for my cabin first. I've given your wife directions in case we get split up.

She gets a tail when she leaves the house. I told her to spend an hour at a friend's house and monitor the guards. They leave after about 15 minutes and return about 15 minutes later. So, she has a 15-minute window to lose them. Fuel is getting low. We need to conserve for the trip. I gave her a radio so we can keep in contact as we make our escape.

Sam wrote back:

Sounds good. I picked up my own tail in the colonel. He's been running with me daily. I have a plan to ditch him the day we escape. Be prepared for an uninvited guest should my plan fail. Non-lethal interference, please. About the fuel: the colonel said Marie could ask for anything and they'd get it for her. She should ask for a fill-up. Tell her not to hesitate to ask for anything else. They owe us. MRE's, Sterno type fuel to cook with, batteries, and anything else she can think of. You can add stuff to the list too. Make them pay for holding me.

I'm ready to go. Let's say four days from now. That will give Marie time to get the fill-up and the supplies. Can you get the truck by then?

Sam handed the notebook back to Josh, and they exchanged a few words about the story. Then Sam talked while Josh read. When he finished, Josh looked at Sam and nodded. *Escape in four days.* Josh ripped out the page and crumpled it up. He flushed it this time, taking the role from Sam. They walked out of the office and Sam said, "See you next time, be careful."

Escape

SAM FINISHED HIS ROUNDS AND WENT BACK TO HIS OFFICE to change into his running gear. He took one last look around. *I'm gonna miss this place*, he thought. For the last eight years this was my second home. But he knew things would only get worse here and the rest of Puyallup. For the safety of him and his family, his only choice was to get to his friends in Ashford. He walked out and closed his office door for probably the last time and said, "I'm going for my run, Nicole."

Before heading outside, he visited Bob. He entered the office, and the secretary waved him on through. Sam knocked on the door a few times and opened it and took a seat in front of Bob's desk. "Bob, I have a favor to ask. I don't want the colonel to run with me today, he's been getting on my nerves in my run is to de-stress. I need time for myself today, can you help?"

Bob took a deep breath and sighed and said, "What would you have me do, Sam?"

"My first hope is that he gets bored waiting for me and find something else to do. Barring that, I'll tell him you have a list of prescriptions for him that you need immediately and he needs to approve."

"I don't think we need anything right now, but I can get with my secretary and see what we can come up with."

"Thanks Bob, I really appreciate this."

Sam stood up and shook Bob's hand then turned and walked out. He made his way to the first floor then walked out to see the colonel did not give up waiting. He walked up and said, "I'm sorry colonel, but Bob needs to see you about some prescriptions. He said to send you right away."

He replied, "We won't be gone long. I'll see to it when we get back."

"I know you're not a doctor, but even you should know patients come first, and the medications are needed. Nobody is here for elective reasons."

"No problem, I'll get my second-in-command on it. Sgt. Murphy, find major Edwards and tell him I said to meet Bob about authorizing some prescriptions."

Defeated, Sam turned to start his run. As the two men jogged off, they could hear Bob screaming from the fifth floor, "Colonel, Colonel! I need to see you immediately!"

Sam thought, *Bob, you brilliant man. I think I might love you!*

The colonel, however, was unfazed. He told Sam, "The major is more than qualified to handle this request."

Sam shook his head in disbelief and ran to Meridian Avenue. From there they headed south and made the customary right turn at the Christian school. After they rounded the corner, they saw a U-Haul van backing into the street.

Josh parked his Bronco between two houses that looked vacant. Then he walked to the curb and waited. About five minutes later a U-Haul van approached, followed by a Ford Mustang. Josh waved and the two vehicles parked on the street in front of him. A short scruffy looking man jumped out of the U-Haul and approached Josh and said, "I got what you need. Do you got what I need?"

Josh pointed to the suitcase and said, "One shiny new AK-47."

He set the suitcase down and opened it to reveal the AK-47. Scruffy picked it up and inspected the weapon and nodded his head. Josh told him he would leave the keys under the seat and the man replied, "Lock the doors, we have a spare key."

"Will do."

Josh got in the truck and waited for the two men to drive off then pulled into a driveway. Then he got in his Bronco and pulled it onto the street, facing south. Sam and his escort would approach from the north. He unlocked the passenger door of his Bronco then got into the U-Haul and waited for Sam to appear. Josh set up the meeting with the supplier about 30 minutes before Sam would arrive, so he had about a 15 to 20-minute wait. Twenty-two minutes later he saw Sam and the colonel come around the corner. *Well that's a downer*, he thought. Josh backed the U-Haul into the street then put the truck in park. Next he put the keys under the seat, opened the door, locked it, and calmly stepped out. He shut the door and waited for the colonel.

Sam looked at the colonel to check his reaction to the U-Haul backing out, hoping he didn't alert the guards. Things would get very messy. As luck would have it, the colonel was lost in his own thoughts and didn't appear to think anything was unusual. The colonel took the lead in going around the truck, with Sam right behind him. When they got to the far side of the truck, Sam gave the old man a gentle nudge, pushing him to the left. Josh fired his taser gun and hit the man on the exposed part of his thigh. The colonel let out a small scream and hit the ground.

Sam looked down at the man and said, "You need to learn to take a hint. I didn't want this to happen, you should have gone to see Bob."

Josh and Sam got in the Bronco and sped south. Half a block later they took a left and made for Meridian. They were only on Meridian for a few seconds before they made a sharp left onto a private driveway. Then it was time for the Bronco to show its stuff and tear through people's yards until they reach 5th St., Southeast where they made a right and a quick left on the 23rd Ave. SE. A block away that turned right on the 7th St., Southeast and sped their way south.

As far as either of the men could tell, nobody was following them. As they sped by the Lowe's store, Josh said we should see your wife on the next block. Sure enough, as they approached the field Sam saw the Blazer on the side of the road. Josh slowed down as they passed so Marie could pull in behind them. When she was on the road, he hit the gas again.

They snaked their way through the back streets always heading south towards Graham, their first checkpoint. They didn't worry about normal traffic because most people didn't have gas anymore. Meeting military vehicles is what worried them. It had been a while since anyone had seen a police officer. They made it past South Hill and the small airfield when Josh tried Meridian again, also known as highway 161 at this point. Just before reaching the highway, Sam spotted a helicopter off to his right. He could only hope it wasn't looking for them. Josh did not share his hope, he knew who the helicopter was looking for Sam. They would have to drive quite a distance before he could hide from helicopters.

When they picked up a tail just before they entered Graham, Josh's feelings were confirmed. Marie radioed ahead and let the men know a Humvee was speeding towards them.

Josh said, "Hold on to your hats ladies and gentlemen, it's going to be a bumpy ride!"

Josh slowed down a little so the Humvee could get closer.

Sam's eyes widened and his heart raced, "What are you doing? We want to get away, not invite them for afternoon tea."

Josh laughed and said, "I've got a surprise in the back. Take the radio and jump back there and then uncover the SAW."

Sam did as instructed and was surprised to see Josh was not joking. There was a fully automatic weapon pointed towards the back and ready to rock 'n' roll.

Josh said, "Radio Marie and tell her we're pulling beside her."

When they were beside the Blazer Josh opened the tailgate window and said, "Aim for the grill and convince them we don't want them following us."

Sam pushed the safety to the firing position, took aim, and sent a few bursts towards the Humvee. The Humvee swerved and drove off the road, but Sam knew he got a few hits in. With the first tail disposed of, the pair of vehicles resumed their race towards Graham.

The helicopter was still following them, however. The two cars still had to rush through Graham and drive several miles before they could ditch the helicopter. Josh thought the best bet was to keep on Meridian through Graham. With the helicopter watching their every move jumping onto the side streets at this point would not do them much good. They got through Graham without incident, surprising both Sam and Josh. But just south of the town two Humvees were blocking the road.

Josh laughed and said, "Do they not see all that open space beside the road? It's not like we're driving sedans."

Josh pulled onto the shoulder and drove around the useless roadblock. Marie followed suit. The two Humvees were soon chasing them. Once again, Josh popped the back window open and Sam took aim. The Humvee drivers were prepared and took evasive action by swerving and driving erratically. *What do they think they're doing? That won't work*, Sam thought. He opened fire, sending several bursts into each vehicle's grill. He intended to disable the vehicles and not kill the occupants. It occurred to Sam that they weren't trying to kill him either. A dead doctor would do them no good.

The swerving allowed the vehicles to deflect some of the rounds. These Humvees had armor, unlike the last one. Sam yelled to Josh, "They're still coming!"

Josh said, "There's a box on the right side wrapped in a comforter. Unwrap it and popped the lid, you'll know what to do."

Sam got the box unwrapped and opened. His eyes widened, and he sucked in a quick breath. His heart froze then pounded. He did not expect to see a box of grenades. When he recovered he said, "Are you kidding me?"

Josh let out a wicked laugh and enjoyed Sam's reaction. He said, "Those are the real deal! Do not throw them out the window, I would hate to have you miss the window and kill us both. Just hold it out the window and let go. If those vehicles are armored as I suspect, you won't do much damage. You will let them know we mean business and may scare them off, or at least take out a tire."

Josh got on the radio and warned Marie about the grenade. He told her not to slow down or stop just, keep driving. Sam grabbed a grenade out of the box and moved closer to the back window. He dangled his arm out the back and pulled the pin. Then he dropped a grenade on the road and jumped back to watch the action. The men driving the Humvees didn't seem to notice what was approaching. As the lead Hummer got within 5 yards of the grenade, it exploded. Sam heard the boom and saw the flash. He and his wife were already too far to take any damage. The Humvees pulled over and stopped the chase. They didn't appear to take any damage but had to reassess the situation.

Sam radioed Marie again and told her to get ready, the turnoff was coming up on the left. The scenery had changed from mostly stores and a few houses to mostly trees and even fewer houses. They were outside of the Graham town boundaries and had just passed the Kapowsin Highway. They were passing a landfill and Josh would make the turnoff into the forest about 1/4 mile past the landfill. He planned to use the cover of the forest to hide from the helicopter. They would head toward Lake Kapowsin and then turned south towards Eatonville.

When the time came, they slowed down and turned into the trees. They couldn't see the helicopter, but they knew it was somewhere above just waiting for them to pop out. The advantage for Josh and company was knowing where they would pop out. The helicopter pilot did not have that information and, therefore, could not send an intercept. Josh's goal was north of Tanwax Lake, and south of Lake Whitman. There were not enough trees between the lakes to cover them. They would be exposed long enough for the helicopter to notice. Josh knew that and had a plan. As the pilot sent an intercept to the east, Josh and company would turn south towards Eatonville. Then they would have to be more careful not to get seen. There were no more major turns between Lake Kapowsin and Eatonville.

Josh made his way to the east side of Ohop Creek and started his southeastern path. He had a hunting cabin behind Eatonville just off the Mashel River. That was their current destination. The pursuit was too hot to try to make it to Ashford today. They were making good progress following Kapowsin Creek. They came to an area in the Surprise Valley where they would have to break cover.

Josh said, "I see two choices here. One, we can make a break for it and hope the helicopter doesn't see us. Or, we can wait until it gets dark. I've got night vision goggles and we can finish the drive lights out, in the cover of darkness."

Sam said, "I vote we wait it out and drive at night. See what my wife thinks."

Josh got on the radio and gave Marie the options.

She said, "There is no reason to risk being seen. We can make a little camp, stretch our legs, and relax for a bit."

Josh agreed and had little choice. Had he disagreed, Sam and Marie would have outvoted him. They shut off their vehicles and everyone stepped out. Viktoriya and Kevin rushed to their father and gave him a big hug. Soon after, their mother joined them. Josh waited a minute and said, "Hey, what about me?"

Viktoriya ran over and gave Josh a big hug saying, "Thank you for helping my father."

Marie also came over and gave him a hug and a kiss on the cheek. Kevin settled for a nod.

Josh said, "All that action made me hungry. We can't make a fire because we can't let the smoke give us away. Marie, pop out one of those sterno cans the Army gave you, and I can boil some water. I've got some food pouches that will do just fine for a quick lunch."

Marie said, "Kevin, come help me. We need to move a few things around to get to the fuel."

"No problem, mom."

Josh fished out a bottle of water in the bucket of food pouches. Sam took his daughter by the hand and walked to the tree line but couldn't see anything interesting. It was just an open field with more trees on the other side. On the plus side, he didn't see a helicopter. They stood watching the sky for a few minutes and caught up with each other before heading back to the group. They were still waiting for the water to boil, Josh and Kevin were trading hunting stories, and Marie had pulled a few chairs from the Blazer. When the water was finally ready, they each picked a "meal" and ate their lunch. Sam wasn't complaining, but it was hard to call his bad food a meal. Compared to Army powdered eggs, however, it was a five-star meal.

When darkness finally arrived, Josh dug out two pairs of night vision goggles. He said, "You still ride with me, Sam? Or do I give these to Marie?"

Marie said, "Sam can take them, I would be a nervous wreck driving without lights. Besides, if Sam gets us both killed, I can blame him for eternity."

Sam said, "Great, no pressure. No pressure at all."

Josh said, "Kevin, I'll need you to ride shotgun. Keep your eyes open and tell me if we are about to drive off a cliff."

Kevin looked confused and said, "Excuse me? What is that supposed to mean?"

"It means I won't have any depth perception while driving with the goggles. Neither will Sam, so your mother will have to do the same for him. It shouldn't be a problem since we can stick to the roads now. In hindsight, it might've been a better idea to hide out in Puyallup and drive the whole way at night. But what's done is done."

Josh and Kevin got in the Bronco and everyone else piled into the Blazer. They turned on the goggles and continued their drive south. Instead of finding a road, they found some rail-road tracks and followed them. The tracks got them to Eatonville, where they got onto a proper road and made their way east to the cabin. It was almost 11 PM when they arrived. Everyone had an MRE along the way and nobody was hungry right now. With the power being out so long, nobody had been up this late in a while and everyone just wanted to sleep. They unpacked a few things and then Josh said, "There's one more thing we gotta do before sleep. Grab your goggles and follow me, Sam."

Josh took Sam behind the cabin into a cliff wall. Then Josh removed some camouflage to reveal a gate in front of the cave. Josh said, "This is why I bought this property. Both vehicles won't fit, so we'll have to work on more camouflage tomorrow. But for now, let's drive in and cover up what we can."

The two men finished hiding their vehicles and went back to the cabin. This was only a small hunting cabin and not meant for so many people. It was a one-room cabin with a fireplace, a wood-burning stove, and a small kitchen area. There were two beds so Josh could invite a hunting buddy. Josh took his bed and Sam and Marie took the other. The two children had to make do on the floor. Soon, everyone was asleep.

Mercy

AT 7 AM SAM WOKE TO HIS iPHONE ALARM - AS DID everyone else. He scrambled for the phone and shut it off. He managed to mumble an apology for waking everyone up and went into the clock settings to turn off the alarm so it wouldn't happen again. He staggered to the wood stove and threw a few logs inside. Josh kept a small pile of wood inside the cabin so he would always have dry wood available. He saw a box of matches above the fireplace mantle and got to work starting the fire.

When the fire was ready, he poured water into a pot and placed it on the stove. While he did that everyone else was taking turns visiting the outhouse. And now it was Sam's turn to make the trip. When he got to the side of the cabin, he looked towards the cave to see if the vehicles were visible. A casual observer might miss the back of the Blazer, but he wouldn't count on it. First thing after breakfast they would have to fix that. When Sam walked out of the outhouse, he could hear a helicopter in the sky. *They haven't given up yet*, he thought.

When he got back inside, he asked if anyone else had heard it and nobody had. They sat in silence contemplating their position until the water was ready. Then the only conversation was what they were choosing for breakfast. Sam eventually broke the silence saying, "We have another decision to make. They're still looking for us, or rather me. Traveling during the day is out of the question, and traveling at night brings other dangers."

Kevin interrupted, "What other dangers? We have the night vision goggles."

Sam said, "Yes, we have the goggles. But others may have them too, including the military. Bad actors tend to come out at night. Without a doubt, it is safer than traveling during the day when the National Guard is hunting me. Here's what I think we should consider: We could wait out the day and drive to Ashford tonight; We could travel now and risk being seen, which is not an option at all, really; Or we can lie low for a few days and see if they give up the hunt.

Josh thought about it for a few minutes and said, "You're right, traveling during the day is not an option. Trusting the goggles that far would not be dangerous. But knowing the military is looking for us and they have better gear than we do, I think the best option is the third option. We should lie low and hang out here for a little while. We can wait them out."

Sam looked at Marie and she said, "I agree with Josh."

Sam said, "That was also my vote. It's the safest of the three options by far. We have more than enough food and we can get more water from the river. Josh and I have friends here in town, so if we need anything else, we know where to look."

Josh said, "Well then, we need to unload supplies from the

vehicles and get them covered again in a hurry. Then we need to work on more camouflage. We need to get on that now."

Everyone got up and headed outside. Josh and Sam backed the vehicles out just far enough so they could reach Josh's tailgate. They made quick work of unloading the vehicles of everything they needed. Sam stationed Viktoriya about 50 yards in front of the cabin as a lookout. After they unloaded everything, Sam and Josh pulled the vehicles forward again and got them covered. Back inside, Josh showed them a little secret. He said, "While this is just a simple hunting cabin, I still gotta be me. Me being me, there's more to the cabin than what you see. He moved near the center of the cabin and stepped on a section of the floor, pushed down with his foot, and slid it forward. A piece of the floor, about 3 feet wide and 5 feet long, slid forward to reveal a storage space.

Josh continued, "It's not a safe room. But it is a nice hiding spot. If anyone comes looking, I want all of you inside. I'll handle whoever comes, they aren't looking for me."

Sam said, "I'm glad you are you. You just took a lot of stress off my shoulders."

Josh smiled and patted his friend on the back and said, "I'm glad I can help. Now let's get to work on the camouflage. We need some good sticks from hardwood trees, some evergreen branches, maybe a few branches from hardwood trees with the leaves still attached. Let's go!"

Marie and Victoria stayed inside and got things unpacked and set up. Josh and Sam armed themselves and Sam pulled out a Glock 9mm with a shoulder holster and told Kevin to suit up. Kevin's eyes lit up, and he took the gift from his father. It's not too often a fourteen-year-old gets to strap on a Glock. Sam said, "Don't get carried away, we need to be careful. Our world is different than it was a few months ago. You shouldn't trust anyone you meet, and they will treat you a lot better when they see you're armed."

They grabbed a few axes, some parachute cord, and each of them attached their knives to their belts. Then they walked out and gathered their materials. After about ten minutes, they decided they had enough sticks and branches to hide the Blazer. Josh tied parachute cord to the top, middle, and bottom section of a long oak stick. Then he tied the other ends to another stick the same size. He pushed each stick into the ground about 6 inches deep on each side of the Blazer. Then they got to work weaving the branches through the parachute cord. When they finished, they went back inside the cabin to help the girls and decide what to do next.

After they finished setting up the cabin, everyone sat down for a talk. The group had enough food with them the last several months, so they weren't too worried about eating. But it was all freeze-dried food and MREs, and that would get boring fast. They needed to keep busy and decided Josh and Sam would go hunting, Kevin and Victoria would go fishing, and Marie would see what food she could gather in the surrounding area. There would be huckleberries for sure, but it was too soon for chestnut. Marie armed herself and Josh picked out a Ruger LC9 for Victoria, lightweight and compact. Perfect for her small frame. Nobody would leave the cabin unarmed. Sam and Marie made sure their children knew how to handle weapons from a young age. But neither had owned their own firearms before.

Everyone started off together, Josh had to show the kids the best place to fish, and Marie wanted to know where they were. When everyone was where they needed to be, Josh and Sam set off for the hunt. They would take whatever they got but were hoping for smaller sized deer. And elk would be more meat than they can handle and they didn't want to waste anything. A moose was out of the question. They were following an old logging road, mostly grown over with grass and ferns. It emptied onto an old road, and they walked it to see if anything might cross. About 100 yards up the road they saw few teenage boys pushing around a slightly younger girl.

They ran to help the girl and as they got closer one boy took a swing. They weren't too sure about what happened next because the young girl was a flurry of motion, and soon both boys were on the ground writhing in pain. As they got closer, they heard the girl say, "I told you to leave me alone. Get up while you can and don't come near me again." Her voice was cold as steel as she spoke. The boys took her advice and ran down the road.

Josh laughed and said, "I would ask if you're okay, but you seem to have the situation under control."

The girl spun around and her eyes widened at the sight of the two men. She asked, "Who are you?"

She took a defensive stance, one foot in front of the other and she leaned on her back foot.

Josh said, "Whoa, tiger. We're not going to hurt you, we ran up to help you. What are you doing out here alone? Can we help you?"

Her eyes narrowed, and she looked both men up and down. She pursed her lips and looked like she would say something but kept quiet. Sam noticed her uneasiness and said, "We're not going to hurt you. We're both well-armed, and if we intended to hurt you, we would've done it already. We're only out here to find a deer."

Her stance didn't change, so Sam tried a different track and said, "Look, I'm a doctor. I've spent my life helping people, not hurting them."

When Sam said "doctor" the girl's eyes widened for a second the narrowed again. She was a small girl, about 5 feet tall, with shoulder-length brown hair and brown eyes.

Sam didn't miss the sign her eyes gave away and said, "Do you need a doctor? I can help you."

The girl lowered her hands, look to the ground, and said, "My parents are sick."

Sam said, "Radiation?"

"No, something else. I'm not sure. They throw up and have diarrhea."

"If you take me there, I'll see what I can do to help. What's your name?"

"Mercy."

She led them down the road a ways and then turned onto a small dirt road. About 50 yards down that road they reached her driveway and then her cabin. Sam told Josh to stay outside so he wouldn't get sick. Then he removed his shirt and placed over his mouth to help prevent him from getting sick. Then he followed Mercy inside. When he entered, he could smell the stink. It overwhelmed his senses, and it surprised him that anyone could live here. Mercy led him to a room in the back and opened the door. He looked inside and saw a man and woman lying on a bed, both gaunt and looked near death.

Sam said, "How long have they been sick?"

Mercy said, "About a week, I think. I try to keep them clean and change out their buckets. Neither of them has eaten in days, and it's all I can do to keep them drinking water."

"I'll do my best, but these two need a hospital. What are their names?"

"Tom and Becky."

Sam introduced himself to his new patients, but they either didn't care or didn't notice. He checked their vitals and pinched their skin in a few places. He asked Mercy why she wasn't sick, and she shrugged. She said, "I don't get sick very often."

"Do you eat the same foods?"

"Almost everything. I don't like pork and most fish. Dad found a pig a few weeks ago, and my parents ate it. I ate none of it."

"Do you know anyone else around here that may be sick?"

"A few people that I know of."

"Your parents probably have a bacterial infection. Or it could be food poisoning if they didn't cook the pig thoroughly. But that probably would've cleared up by now, so I'm leaning toward infection. I have a few antibiotics back in my cabin. I'll return here shortly with medicine. Both your parents are dehydrated, so you'll have to work harder at getting water down their throats. When I get back, I'll need you to take me to the other sick people."

Mercy nodded her head, and Sam walked outside.

Sam told Josh he would have to hunt alone because he needed to get back to the cabin for his medical bag. Then he was going to make a few rounds.

Settling In

SAM VISITED A FEW MORE HOMES WITH VERY SICK occupants. They all had one thing in common—they all got a pig from the same farm. Sam went to visit the farm and took Josh with him in case the farmer didn't like what he heard. Sam had to tell the farmer he couldn't let people eat his infected pigs. Sam asked the farmer why he wasn't sick, and the man said, "It's pretty simple, I don't eat pork." The pair left with an uneasy feeling. Neither of them believed the farmer would stop trading his pigs.

With so many new patients, Sam said he couldn't just leave. Everyone in the small group agreed to stay in Eatonville as long as it took to get everyone healthy. They would need to make the cabin more comfortable for the longer stay. The two children were still sleeping on the floor with nothing but the sleeping bag underneath them. The outhouse was fine, but they didn't have a shower. The only way to bathe at the moment was to take a dip in the river. With the current layout, there was no privacy for changing clothes.

Kevin went outside together small pieces of wood for the stove. He collected a few nice pieces and through the trees, he could see a Humvee approaching. He dropped his load and ran for the cabin. Then he burst through the door and everyone looked to see what the ruckus was about. They saw Kevin breathing heavy, his face pale white. He said, "Humvee...coming...now."

Sam and Josh moved like a swift, efficient team. Josh got the hideaway opened and Sam tossed the sleeping bags down with the bedding from his bed. Then the family jumped into the pit. Josh added a few more bags to make it appear he was alone in the cabin. A minute later there was a knock at the door and Josh summoned up his best behavior. He opened the door with a smile and a slow hello. One soldier returned his greeting and said, "Are there any others with you?" Both soldiers peered around Josh to see for themselves.

Josh said, "It's just me. I left the city last week and am still trying to get comfortable here."

"We're looking for a black Chevy Blazer and its owner. He's traveling with his wife and two teenage children, a boy and a girl. Have you seen them?"

"No, I've only seen two other people since I got here. A young girl in an old man."

When telling a lie, it's good to throw in a little truth to throw off your interrogator. He saw a young girl and an old man in the farmer. The soldier who did all the talking nodded his head and thanked Josh for his time. They turned around and looked around the cabin. Josh got a little nervous and retrieved his AR-15. He hoped the camouflage was as good as he thought it was as he watched them through the window. After a long thirty seconds, the men got back in the Humvee and drove away. Josh slid the floor open about a foot to let in some air and light. He said, "Let's wait about five minutes to be sure they aren't coming back." Josh watched out the front window and hoped the men left for good. He had the family wait for ten minutes instead of five and finally gave the okay.

Sam said, "I guess lying low was a good idea. I'm a little shocked at putting so much time and resources to bring back one man."

Josh said, "That colonel may feel betrayed, and the little ticked off about getting tased."

"I told him at the start he wasn't my friend. I also did my best to keep him from going running that day. It is off my conscience."

"You don't have to convince me. Besides, I've always wanted to tase someone!"

Sam looked at his friend like he was crazy and shook his head. Then they both laughed.

They retrieved their belongings from the hole and put everything back where they belonged. Sam and Josh needed to contact Paul Peterson again to let them know about their delay, but the soldiers got them spooked a little. They weren't able to put the solar panels on or near the cabin because of the dense forest. They planned to walk to an open field or meadow and set up a temporary location to send a message. Sitting out in the open with soldiers looking for Sam and his family was risky. Sam also wanted to check on his patients, but again that would be risky today. The family would need to stick close to the cabin. It was up to Josh to spread the word Sam wouldn't be making rounds today. They would wait until tomorrow to message Paul.

Josh grabbed his favorite hunting rifle just in case he saw a deer and walked out the door. He made his way to Mercy's home and knocked on the door. Mercy answered and she scrunched her eyebrows at seeing Josh. She said, "Where's the doctor?"

"He can't make it today for personal reasons. He's really sorry and will be here tomorrow. How are your parents?"

"I can't tell for sure, but I think they're a little better today. Those pills may be starting to work."

"That's good to hear. Would you be able to let the others know about Sam? I don't know where everyone lives."

"Sure, no problem."

Josh thanked the young girl and went looking for some meat.

⚜

The next day, they deemed it safe to walk about without the risk of seeing anyone from the military. It wouldn't take two days to canvass an area as small as Eatonville. Sam kept the same routine as the hospital and made his rounds to the patients in the morning. When he finished, he and Josh picked up a few solar panels, laptop, and small satellite modem. There was a small open meadow nearby where they could set up and catch enough sunlight to fire up the satellite receiver. The laptop had a full charge and would not hook up to the solar panels. Doing so could cause problems.

They got set up and fired up the modem. Then Sam turned on the laptop and got connected. Then he sent another message to Paul:

Paul,

We got out of Puyallup and hunkered down at Josh's cabin in Eatonville. The military still looking for me. Too dangerous to move. There are a lot of sick people here and I'll stay until they're healthy before moving on. Need supplies. Can you put me in contact with Eatonville group? I'm not sure how long we'll be here.

Josh added his address to the message so the Eatonville contact could find them.

The men packed up their equipment and headed back to the cabin. When they got inside, Marie was the only one there. Sam said, "Where are the kids?"

She said, "Kevin went out to hunt because he wants real meat and Viktoriya went with him because she was bored. They left about thirty minutes ago."

Sam shot Josh a look, and Josh understood the unspoken language. Josh said, "I'm going to go find that thing I was looking for earlier."

Marie's mouth hung open, and she blushed. Josh picked up a rifle and walked out the door.

Kevin and Viktoriya walked down the path as quiet as they could. About 100 yards away they saw three deer. Kevin moved slow and quiet, then raised the rifle to his eye. He flipped the safety as he brought the rifle up. Then took aim at the smallest of the three, heeding his father's advice. They didn't want to waste any meat. He took in a slow deep breath and exhaled slow and steady while pulling the trigger. The young deer fell. The other two ran off so fast that Kevin didn't see which way they went. They ran up to the fallen deer and field dressed it. Both teens were experienced hunters and knew what they needed to do. Viktoriya would rather fish, however.

When they finished, they began the walk back to the cabin. Kevin lagged behind because he was dragging the deer, he had handed the rifle to his sister so he wouldn't be as heavy. Viktoriya didn't realize how far ahead she had got. She turned around and didn't see her brother and backtracked to find him. When he came into view, she saw a man talking to him, or arguing. She saw the man push her brother down and grab the deer.

She raised the rifle, flipped the safety off, and said, "Put that deer down and walk away."

The man looked up and saw a young girl with a rifle pointed at him. For a moment he didn't move or breathe, then he took in the size of his adversary and felt bold.

"You won't shoot me over this dear. You can find another one."

Viktoriya fired and put a round an inch from his left foot. The man jumped, and she fired again but put the second round an inch from his right foot. Then she said, "If you don't put that deer down and walk away right now, the next one goes between your eyes."

The man's ashen face said what his words could not. He dropped the deer, turned and ran. Kevin got up, looked at his sister and said, "Who are you and what did you do with my sister? When did you learn to be so hard?"

She shrugged and said, "I saw it on TV once."

Kevin shook his head. He grabbed his deer and the two started their walk home again. This time Viktoriya stayed close to her brother. When they got home, they repeated the story of the hunt and the man who tried to steal the deer. Sam asked Kevin why he was unarmed. He said he didn't take his pistol because he had a rifle.

Sam said, "From now on, you don't leave the cabin without a sidearm. Even if you have your rifle for hunting, take the pistol with you. That goes for everyone here. Everybody's getting hungry and desperate. Now let's get your deer hung."

◈◈◈

Two days later, two armed men approached the cabin while Josh was out front chopping wood. He looked up and said, "Can I help you?" One man identified himself as Richard and said, "I'm looking for Sam and Josh. Paul Peterson sent us."

Josh smiled and stuck his hand out and said, "I'm Josh, Sam is inside. Come with me and we'll go inside for a chat."

Richard looked to be in his 30s, he had short cropped hair and a bushy mustache and beard. He wore a John Deere cap, jeans, and a T-shirt that said, "Who Farted?"

He introduced his friend as Matt. Matt was barely in his 20s, clean-shaven, with blonde hair that almost touched his shoulders. Josh introduced the two men to everyone else. Richard asked if they should go somewhere else to talk and Sam said, "We're fine here, nobody is keeping any secrets."

Richard nodded and asked, "So how can we help you?"

Sam said, "We were headed to Ashford but had to stop here

because the National Guard wants to take me back to the hospital. I'm a doctor and they were holding me prisoner there since the first attack. But, there are so many sick people here that I couldn't just leave. We have enough food to last a few months, but nothing fresh. Well, except the deer my son got a few days ago. All of our long-term gear is out at our cabins in Ashford."

Richard and Matt looked at each other out of the corner of their eyes when Sam said he was a doctor. Richard said, "You're a doctor? What are they doing with all of you? All of ours are gone."

Sam said, "Gone? What do you mean, gone?"

"A Chinook helicopter flew into town and all the doctors and nurses were gathered up, packed into the helicopter, and nobody saw them again. The soldiers told us the doctors and nurses were needed to help the affected cities, and would be back soon. It's been four weeks."

Sam shook his head in disbelief. He said, "I think they're still looking for me, but I don't know why they're wasting all the time on one man. It makes little sense to me. It makes me grateful that I had a friend who could get me out. I am curious about where the doctors went, however. I can't believe they left you without a doctor, do you know people who need a one?"

Richard said, "There are a lot of sick people. Some probably can't be helped, like old Mr. Jeffries. The doctors said he had cancer before the attack. We don't have anything here that could help him, even with you here. But there are some who would need your help. How long are you planning to stay?"

"Originally, just a few days. When we thought the Army wasn't looking for me anymore, we were going to head on to

Ashford. Then I found all the sick people, and we decided to stay longer. Which reminds me, there's an old farmer about 1/2 mile away who was selling sick pigs. You should tell everyone not to buy anything from Mike Bunner. I don't think he was sincere when he said he would stop selling them himself."

Richard said, "Well, we can help you with basic supplies and get you a little more comfortable. Tell me what you need."

Sam said, "If you have two cots or small beds, I'm sure my children would like to get off the floor. If you have anything where we can build a small privacy wall, my wife and daughter would probably thank you. Until then, they can change when all the men are out of the cabin. If anyone can spare some fresh vegetables, that would be great."

Sam, Josh, and Marie finished the wish list. Richard said he would take it to the group and they would put together what they could. Sam asked about the sick people and asked if there was a hospital in town. Richard said, "only a Multi-Care clinic." Sam said that would do and asked Richard to have anyone needing care to be there in two days at around 2 PM. He would need someone to take him there so he didn't get lost. If anyone was too sick to go there, he would get to them later. He also asked to have lookouts, so he didn't get surprised by any soldiers looking for him.

They agreed that anyone who could afford it would leave a donation of fresh or canned vegetables, meat, or even fresh-water. The river provided all the water they needed, but they needed to treat it first.

For the next few months, Sam took care of the patients in

Eatonville in the vicinity of Josh's cabin. They had a steady supply of vegetables and fresh meat throughout the summer. As winter approached, the meat got scarce. The vegetables went from fresh to canned, but nobody complained. Kevin and Viktoriya did most the hunting and fishing, Josh pitched and when he could. Josh played bodyguard to Sam as he made his rounds.

Winter

THE TIME PASSED AND WINTER ARRIVED. WHAT STARTED AS a short-term hiding spot turned into a months-long stay. The current plan was to stick out the winter in Eatonville then move on to Ashford in the spring. But things took a turn for the worse. People were starving and the game was getting scarce. Kevin and Viktoriya came home from hunting empty-handed again.

Kevin said, "Dad, we walked at least 3 miles out and saw nothing. Not even a rabbit."

Sam said, "It's the same all around. Nobody has meat to spare and I'm working for free nowadays. It doesn't bother me and we won't starve. Not anytime soon, anyway."

Josh said, "If the food has left us, we need to go to the food. Maybe we should scrap the plan to stay the winter here and move on to Ashford."

"Marie and I have been discussing that. I hate to leave anyone here without a doctor, but our friends need a doctor too. But

I think we should try to stick it out a little longer. There are a few people I'd hate to abandon at this time."

Josh was about to say something, but a knock at the door stopped him. Instead, he got up and opened the door and saw a young girl with short brown hair and tears in her eyes.

He said, "Mercy, what's wrong? Please come in."

Mercy said, "My mother is sick again. Could you please come look at her, Sam?"

Sam stood up and said, "Of course, Mercy. Just let me get my coat and bag and will be on our way. Josh, do you mind tagging along?"

"Of course not. I'm right behind you."

As they were walking to Mercy's home, Sam asked her, "What is wrong with her?"

Mercy replied, "She has a fever, she's throwing up again, and her belly hurts."

Sam asked, "How long has she been this way?"

Mercy thought for a second and said, "It started two days ago. She woke up in the morning with the pain."

"Is your father sick again too?"

"I haven't seen my father in a week. He left to go hunting and never came back."

Sam and Josh looked at each other upon hearing that news. Nobody is going to abandon their family at a time like this with nowhere to go. Whatever happened to her father, it was bad. Sam thought it could be anything from a cougar to someone killing him for his gun. Either way, it was unlikely

Mercy would see her father again. While various scenarios were playing in Sam's head, they reach their destination.

They walked in and Josh noticed it smelled a lot better than last time. Sam and Mercy went into the bedroom and Sam got to work. He felt her forehead and knew she had a fever but pulled the thermometer out to get an accurate reading. While he was waiting on the thermometer, he took her pulse and checked her blood pressure. Then he said, "Ma'am, where does it hurt?"

He wasn't sure she heard him until she pointed to the right side of her belly. He pulled the thermometer out of her mouth and it read 102°. Her pulse was weak and slow in her blood pressure was normal but on the low side.

Sam took Mercy out of the bedroom and said, "I think she has appendicitis. I will have to operate to remove the appendix and I have to do it now. I have no way to put her to sleep, so she will feel everything. I will need you to hold her down and keep her still."

Mercy and Josh nodded their heads and the three walked into the room. Mercy's mother was still, and her face no longer showed pain. All three of them knew it was too late. Mercy's eyes welled up with tears and she ran to her mother and laid next to her and hugged her.

Sam and Josh walked out of the room to give Mercy her privacy. A few minutes later she walked out of the room and asked, "What am I going to do? My father disappeared and my mother has died, I'm all alone."

Sam said, "The first thing we'll do is give your mother a proper burial. Then you can join us, we could use another strong hand. Go pack everything you need. Josh and I will find some shovels and dig a grave."

The two men walked outside and found a shovel and a pickax in the shed. Mercy walked out while they were digging and watched. She said, "I can't sit in there knowing my mother is dead in the next room."

Josh said, "We'll be done here in a few minutes. We'll put her to rest and get on our way."

They carried Mercy's mother outside and lowered her into the hole. Mercy said a few words and thanked her mom for being a good mother. While Sam and Josh were covering the grave, Mercy walked around and gathered a few stones. With the grave covered, she arranged the stones to say "Mom." They went inside to gather her things and Sam told Mercy to write a short note for her father in case he returned. Sam knew the father would not return, but he thought it might help the young girl say goodbye.

⚜

When they returned home Sam's family was surprised to see Mercy with them. Sam said, "Mercy will stay with us, at least for a while. Is there room for her on your bed, Viktoriya?"

He gave his daughter a look that said, "say yes," and she knew that was the only answer.

Viktoriya smiled and said, "Yes, of course."

Sam told Mercy she could unpack her things and showed her where she could put them. Viktoriya offered to help in the two teens got to work moving her in. Mercy pulled out a trophy and Viktoriya told her she should put it on the fireplace mantle. Kevin looked at it and said, "Cool, what did you get that for?"

She said, "I got that from my first Krav Maga tournament.

78

My father was my instructor, and he was surprised that I won. He was proud, but surprised."

Josh said, "Ah, so that's what you used to beat the crap out of those two boys when we first met you."

"Yes, I defended myself with Krav Maga."

Josh was looking out the window at the river when he saw movement. He told everyone to be quiet and asked Sam to get his Remington. Sam knew they were safe when he asked for a hunting rifle and not his AR-15. Sam handed him the rifle and a few .270 rounds. Sam loaded a round and opened the door as quiet as possible, then stepped outside. He took aim at a massive elk on the riverbank. A few seconds later everyone was running to the riverbank to claim their prize. Josh dressed the big elk and told Kevin to run back and grab a hatchet and a few saws. This beast was too heavy to drag in one piece. They would clean it and quarter in place and then get the meat to the cabin.

Sam said, "Josh, you and Victoria can handle the cleaning and quartering. That is a lot of meat. Why don't Kevin and I go get Richard and have him take most of this meat to donate around town."

Josh said, "That's fine with me. Tell him to bring a horse or two, and a wagon."

An hour later Sam and Kevin returned with Richard and a few other men. They brought a wagon pulled by a horse. Josh walked out of the cabin and said, "Good evening men, it's a fine day for a barbecue!"

The men laughed and waved their hello's.

Josh continued, "The meat is waiting for you right there. That's almost a whole elk. I kept enough for three days.

That's all I think it will last at the current temperature. For once in my life, I wish it was a lot colder and we could freeze the meat outside. Instead, we only have a refrigerator.

The men loaded up the elk one piece at a time. Each 1/4 piece of the elk weight about 100 pounds, maybe more. There were three of those and then the leftovers from the piece Josh cut up for the family. Richard said, "Thanks for the meat, we appreciate it. I hate to take the gift and run, but it will be dark soon, so we need to head out."

Josh said, "No worries, we understand."

❦

A week had passed since Mercy moved in. Nobody had seen another game animal since Josh took the elk. Even after gifting most the meat to the townsfolk, a few people had died of starvation. Sam, Marie, and Josh discussed moving on to Ashford again. They couldn't rely on a lucky elk to keep them fed. After discussing the pros and cons for about an hour, the three decided it was time to move on. They didn't have to break the news to the children because they were all in the same room and heard everything, of course. Everyone packed their bags and prepared to leave the next morning.

Morning came, and they each had an MRE for breakfast. Sam and Josh uncovered the vehicles and pulled them out of the cave to the front of the cabin. In short order, both vehicles were loaded up and ready to go. Josh locked up the cabin, and they drove to see Richard. Richard was sad to see them go but understood. He asked Sam, "How are you doing on gas? Can you make it to Ashford?"

"It will be close, but I think I'll make it. Being chased here by Humvees and helicopters used more gas than we expected."

"Well, you're in luck. I live next to the gas station because I own the gas station. Pull your vehicles up to the pumps and I'll get you filled up. You have certainly earned it."

Josh and Sam thanked Richard and pulled up to the pumps. It took Richard a few minutes to turn everything on. He explained they were working with solar power. He also said the gas was old, but it would work. After they filled the tanks of both trucks, they said goodbye to Richard again and thanked him for the gas. Richard told him to say "Hi" to Paul for him, and if they ever need anything, all they had to do was ask.

The two vehicles pulled out and made their way to Ashford. It felt strange driving and not being chased. It also felt strange to be the only vehicles on the road. They drove through Elbe and were surprised to see people moving around. The people were equally surprised to see vehicles on the road. Sam was thankful the people didn't harass him and Josh. A few minutes later they were in Ashford and didn't see anyone on the streets, or anywhere. Already a tiny little spot on the highway, it now looked like a ghost town. They made a left turn off the highway and made their way to Paul's house.

They pulled into the driveway and got out of the vehicles. Paul came rushing out of the house and said, "Thank God! You have perfect timing, scrub up!"

Part II The Park

Winter Planning

JACK AND DIANE GATHERED WOOD OUT IN THE COLD woods while Ralph and Brandon went hunting. There was fresh snow on the ground and Jack hoped it wouldn't stay long. The winter has treated them well so far. They kept the cottage warm and their bellies full. Having three experienced hunters was a major benefit. Diane was still learning but catching on quick. A person learns faster when starvation is on the line.

Diane asked, "When do we leave for the meeting?"

Jack said, "In about an hour. Once we collect enough wood, we can have a little snack and then head out."

They each collected an armload and made it back to the cottage. Jack's German Wirehaired Pointers, Basha and Mercedes, waited until they dropped their loads then gave their customary greeting. They jumped up and gave hugs and kisses. Jack grabbed a towel and dried his face. Diane went into the kitchen and put together a little snack.

Just then, Ralph burst into the door and said, "You gotta see this!" Jack put his coat and hat back on and walked outside to see what Ralph was excited about. When he got outside, Brandon was standing next to a very large blacktail buck. Brandon held up the head and Jack counted seven points on one side and eight on the other.

"That's a mighty big buck you got there, Brandon. Congrats!"

"Thanks, I took them with my bow. I had to wait for it to get into range. I couldn't believe it when the buck kept walking towards me. I thought for sure he'd catch my scent and run."

"I'd help skin him, but Diane and I must get to a meeting."

"Don't worry about it, dad and I got this."

Ralph said, "Yeah, this will be a problem. If the weather stays freezing, we can store the meat outside in the shed. We'll be able to take our time eating it all."

Jack said, "And here I've been praying the snow would go away and it will get warmer. I like your idea."

Jack went back inside to have his snack with Diane. They finished up and got dressed for the cold once again. They stepped outside, waved to father and son, and started their hike to the meeting location. If they walk fast, they can make it in thirty minutes... without the snow. Jack estimated it would take them about forty-five minutes now. They discussed chores and who would do each over the next week. Ralph isn't much of a cook, so he takes on more cleaning duties. Brandon is okay in the kitchen and is taking lessons. Jack is the best of the three cooks by far, and everyone would prefer he cooked every day. Jack would rather not.

Everyone hunted. All four of them take firearms but try to

take the game with bows. They can reuse arrows, ammo not so much. But if they're hungry, and can't get within range of an animal, they will use the rifle. It's also a bad idea to go anywhere unarmed. Especially if you're dragging a fresh kill behind you. They gather wood daily to keep their rotation going. The fresh load goes in the shed to dry out. Then they take a load for the shed into the cottage. The new load goes at the end of the line and will spend a few days there before making it to the fire.

Diane was in better shape now, Jack didn't need to slow down for her anymore. They always went walking for one reason or another, even if it's only to exercise. They made it to the meeting location in only forty minutes. They crested the hill, but this time Paul was not there to greet them. He ditched the cold weather and waited inside. They walked into the cabin-like structure and Paul rose to his feet to shake their hands.

Paul said, "Jack, good to see you! And Diane, it's always a pleasure to see your beautiful smile."

Diane smiled and said, "And I'll never get tired of your compliments."

Jack just shook his head and smiled.

Paul had already set up the tables and chairs and got a fire started. Jack believes in getting everywhere early, but Paul takes it to a new level. The only thing they could do was sit and wait for everyone else to show up. Jason Keller showed up about five minutes after Jack and Diane. Soon Mark Wilson and Brett Donaldson had arrived. Nikki and the rest filled the seats, and the meeting got started.

Paul stood and said, "Welcome. I'm glad everyone could make

it. We have a lot to discuss so I'll start with Elbe. I spoke with Ranger John this morning via radio to get caught up on the situation there. It's going good for the most part, better than I expected. There are a few people who made a show of helping but did nothing. In return, nobody has helped them. They are causing trouble now, trying to steal food from the people who put in the work."

Jack asked, "Is anyone doing anything about the slackers?"

Paul responded, "John is still in touch with his fellow Rangers in Elbe and Ashford. They're all deputized, not that it matters too much anymore, but they will handle the thieves."

Jack said, "That's good to hear. I hate thieves."

Paul continued, "Yes, don't we all. Diane, you'll be glad to hear that your favorite two former punks have improved so much that John rewarded them by giving their guns back."

Diane didn't say anything. The news tore at her. She was happy they turned it around, but still didn't like them.

Then Paul said, "They've been very helpful finding food and helping the seniors winterize their homes. John has been in law enforcement long enough to know if they were just playing along. I don't think the two kids could pull one over on him."

Diane smiled and nodded her head, but inside she was still divided.

Paul went on to a new topic and explained how Jason and Mark were spending a lot of time keeping the cabins of Sam and Josh looking lived in. They lived closest to the respective cabins and kept the place is looking lived in. Paul had the spare keys for everyone's cabin locked up in his home. Some days they'd make a fire in the fireplace and others they would work outside on small projects. The idea was to keep squatters away. Paul knew Sam and Josh would arrive in the spring, but he kept it to himself. If anything happened to the pair before they arrived, the rest of the group would still think they were just missing. Everyone here had their own worries. There is no need to say they were safe until they were here. Paul had an idea to keep the places lived in without sending people there to put on a show.

Paul said, "Sam and Josh still haven't made it here and we've been keeping their cabins looking lived in and clean. Jason and Mark have been doing a great job of it, but it sucks a lot of their time. We picked up a few extra people, and I thought it would be a good idea to put Robin and her family in one cabin, and Jack's friends in the other. Robin can take Sam's cabin and Ralph can move into Josh's. If the two men show up, will figure out what to do then."

Nikki said, "That sounds like a great idea. Although, I'd miss my new friend. She makes good company and her son is a big help around the cabin. But I'm sure they'd all like more room and a little privacy."

Jack nodded and said, "I know Ralph and Brandon would love to get out of their tiny room and have more space. They've never complained, but sleeping on that couch bed cannot be too comfortable. I have no doubt they would love the idea."

Paul said, "Great. Have the two families get packing and we will move them in two days. Now that that's settled, how is everyone doing? Does anyone need any assistance?"

This was the time for anyone to bring up issues they were having. Nobody needed help yet. But Brett said he ran into someone he hadn't seen before hunting near his property, just outside the park boundaries. The man didn't look too friendly but didn't say anything or make any threatening moves.

Brett said, "I said nothing to him, but I didn't trust him. My gut said to keep an eye on him, so I hung back and spied on the man. I followed him across the park boundary for about half a mile before returning home. I think he's made a home in the park and tried his luck hunting further away. Maybe seeing me will keep them inside the park, but I don't think so. I think he will be back."

Jack said, "I used to hear a lot of shots coming from the park, but now I don't hear them very often. I wrote it off to either out of animals or out of ammo. We hunt inside the park and I haven't noticed a big reduction in animals yet. It could be they've pushed the animals toward us. If so, I thank them. But if they're following the animals, that may cause issues."

Paul said, "Okay, every one be diligent and keep your eyes open when hunting in or near the park. I don't want anyone to get shot over an animal. We can't keep them from hunting so we will need to be careful. Does anyone have anything else?"

Nobody brought up any issues so Paul said, "Great. Everyone meet at my house in two days at noon. I'd like everyone to help get the families moved in. Nikki and Jack, if your people have too much stuff to carry, let me know and I'll send a horse and carriage."

Nikki and Jack nodded their heads and everyone stood to leave.

Jack, Diane, and Jason stayed back to help clean up. It only took about five minutes and Paul thanked the three for their help and they walked out and locked up. Jason walked with Jack and Diane as usual. They discussed hunting and where they were finding the most game. Jack said they were doing best in the park and Jason said he¹ leaned that way himself. Jason said, "It's like the animals know it's open season. They aren't as cocky as they used to be." Jason and Jack laughed at that and Diane just smiled. The men were experienced hunters and knew the joke. You always see elk during deer season and deer during elk season. It's much harder to find an elk during elk season or a deer during deer season.

They came to Jason's turnoff, and the three said their good-byes. Now that they were alone, Diane asked if they should worry about the hunter Brett had seen.

Jack said, "I don't think we need to worry about that one. He would have to go far out of his way to get to us. But he's not the only person in the park. I'm sure a lot of them have died since we were last there and more will die this winter. But the ones who can hunt will survive and if they are pushing the animals this way, we do need to worry about them. Not for the obvious reason of competition for game, but how they view us as competition. I don't mind sharing, but do they? That's the real issue."

The two walked in silence the rest the way home. When they arrived, Basha and Mercedes ran up to greet their friends. They were outside with Brandon guarding the deer hanging from the tree. Brandon had built a little campfire to keep everyone warm. Jack greeted Brandon and said, "Let's got inside for a minute, we've got some good news for you."

They took off their coats and gloves before telling Brandon and Ralph they were moving. Father and son seemed excited but also looked like they were holding back.

Jack said, "I thought you would be happier to be getting a bed."

Ralph nodded and said, "I'm happy for the bed for sure. But it's been fun living with you, and I'll miss you and the dogs."

Brandon nodded in agreement.

Jack laughed and said, "Well, it's not like won't ever see each other again. You know where I live. Start packing your things tomorrow, we'll leave in two days."

Moving In

THE HORSE AND WAGON ARRIVED AT JACK'S COTTAGE AT 9 AM. Ralph decided to leave his car with Jack. He didn't have much fuel left so taking it was a risk. While Ralph and his son didn't have much, what they had was big and heavy. Besides clothing, they had rifles, handguns, bows, a shotgun, and all the various equipment and ammo for said weapons. Jack supplied them with some food so they wouldn't starve while they settled in. Besides meat from Brandon's big buck, Jack gave them some of his canned vegetables and a few meal pouches. He told them not to hesitate to ask if they needed anything else.

When the wagon was all loaded up, they walked to Paul's. The trip would only take a few hours, so Jack left the dogs at the cottage. They would arrive long before noon and Jack didn't mind. It would give him time to talk to Paul and relax. It would take longer to get to Paul's with the wagon since they couldn't take any of the shortcuts. They would travel all by road. The scene looked like something out of an old West movie, minus the paved roads. A bunch of armed men and a woman walking on either side of the wagon with rifles slung over shoulders.

They arrived at Paul's about an hour later. Paul was outside to greet them, and Larry came to unhitch the horse and take her back to the stables. He would bring out a fresh horse when they were ready to leave. Paul said, "Get inside, all of you. It's too cold to be standing around chitchatting."

Brandon said, "I'll stay out here and watch our stuff."

Paul admired Brandon's youthful determination but said, "Your stuff will be fine. We can see the wagon from where we will be sitting. I don't get too many visitors, well, I don't see too many strangers. If anyone tried to steal anything, they would make it five steps before they died of lead poisoning."

Brandon smiled and said, "Okay."

About thirty minutes later another wagon pulled up with the belongings of Robin, her husband Mark, and their son Jay. Nikki was with them. They all came inside and Paul made the introductions. Over the next hour, everyone else had arrived to help with the move. They didn't need all these people for the actual move, they needed them for protection. Each family was traveling with all their belongings. Today, that meant necessities. Everything they had was valuable to survive and anyone who saw them would want it. The armed escort was a show of force.

When everyone arrived, they all went outside and waited for Larry to finish hitching the horses. They would go to Sam's cabin first to drop off Robin and her family. Sam had a son and daughter and his cabin was bigger than Josh's. Josh was still single but was smart enough to build a cabin with more than one room. A few minutes later Larry said the horses were ready and the large group made their way to Sam's cabin.

When they arrived, Jason and Brett went before everyone else to make sure the cabin was empty. They gave the all clear in the group join them. Jason showed the family around and helped them settle in. They got the belongings off the wagon and into the respective rooms. Sam's cabin was bigger than most, and had a spacious living room with a fireplace and a wood-burning stove. In that aspect, it matched his home in Puyallup, but the similarities ended there. Instead of a large window in the living room, he had several smaller windows. All the floors were wood instead of carpet. There were no ceiling lights in the cabinet all. All the lighting was from lamps. With the electrical grid down, there was no electricity coming into the cabin. Neither Paul nor Jason knew where Sam kept his solar equipment.

The kitchen area had a well with a pump for easy access to water. There was no dishwasher in this cabin. There was a large double sink, making washing dishes by hand much easier. Cooking without electricity could be done on the wood-burning stove and the fireplace. The master bedroom had a queen-sized bed, dresser, and armoire. The other two bedrooms matched, but with twin beds. Jay chose Kevin's room because Viktoriya's looked too girly. When they got everything inside, the group moved on to Josh's cabin to get Ralph and Brandon settled in.

They took more than thirty minutes to get to the cabin and once again, Jason and Brett scouted the cabin out. This time, however, they signaled everybody to stay back and the two men returned to the group. Jason said, "I saw people inside."

Brett said, "They couldn't have been there long. I was just here three days ago."

Paul said, "We move in and knock on the door. Will give them the chance to leave on their own."

The group moved up the driveway to the cabin. Paul and Jason walked up to the door. Everyone else took up defensive positions just in case things went bad. Paul knocked on the door and stepped back and to the side. He waited thirty seconds and tried again, but nobody answered the door. Paul mustered up his best authoritative voice and said, "We know you're in there, and it's time for you to leave. We are giving you the chance to walk away. This is not your home, so you can open the door and walk out, or we're coming in."

Paul waited about a minute and still the door didn't open. He pulled out the keys to unlock the door and opened it. Then he jumped to the site again but was too slow. Paul took a round in his arm, near the shoulder. Brandon was behind the wagon and had taken aim at the door with his .270 Winchester. He saw the man crouched on one knee and took aim. Brandon hit the man center mass. Mark Wilson, the group's medic, ran to help Paul. He and Jason got away from the cabin behind the carriage.

Jack took over as spokesman and said, "That was the wrong answer." Jack moved for the door and motioned for everyone to follow. When he got to the door, he peeked inside and saw no one except the man Brandon had shot, and he wasn't moving. He moved inside and Jason came in right behind him. Jack scooped up the man's .38 Special. Everyone but Nikki and Mark soon followed. Nikki was too old for that and helped Mark with Paul.

The living room was clear, and Jack opened the first door he saw, on the right, and jumped back. He waited a few seconds and peeked in. He saw no one in this room, but he and Jason went inside to clear it just in case. They repeated the process for the door on the left. That turned out to be the bathroom, and it was clear. There is one more door further down on the right. That would be the second bedroom. Once again, Jack opened it and jumped back.

"Don't shoot!"

Jack told the person, "Come out slowly with your hands on top your head. Don't do anything stupid and you walk away."

The woman said, "We don't have any guns. It's just my son and me."

Jack said, "You come out first, hands on head. Then your son."

The woman came out first as instructed. Jack saw a young woman with shoulder length red hair. Her lips trembled and her eyes darted from one person to the next. She didn't know how many had come to the door until now. She realized how stupid her husband was to try to fight for the cabin. Her son walked out next with his hands on his head. He was a young man of about six or seven years with chestnut hair and brown eyes. His face was a mask and Jack could not tell if the boy was scared or mad. *Maybe a little of both*, he thought.

They walked mother and son to the living room and set them on the couch. Jason and Brett drug the body outside so the mother and son wouldn't have to look at him. Jack asked their names.

The woman said, "I'm Julie, and this is my son, Prince."

"Why didn't you just leave when we told you to?"

"I didn't see anyone outside. My husband told us to get into the room and hide. What he did, he did on his own."

"I hate to tell you this, but you can't stay. You need to pack up your belongings and get moving."

Someone followed Julie and Prince around the cabin as they gathered their things. They saw the broken window on the backside of the living room and knew that's how the family got in. They probably had the boy crawl through the window and unlocked the front door. They would board the window up for now and see about repairing it later. They would also need to find bars to cover the windows.

Julie said, "This is everything we have, I guess we'll be going now. Can you tell us how to get to the national park?"

Jack said, "I'll walk you out and give you directions."

They walked out and passed the body. Prince looked at his father on the ground staring at the sky, and his eyes welled with tears. Now Jack had no problem seeing the anger in the little boy's face. Jack gave the woman directions to the park and wished her well. Prince said, "Can I have my father's gun?"

"I'm sorry young man, but that is not going to happen. Your father shot my friend with that gun and we're keeping it. I will not give anyone a second chance to shoot my friends with the same gun."

Prince scowled and gave Jack the best stink eye he could muster. Jack looked at the boy and held back a smile. Instead, he tried to give the young man some advice.

"Always think before you act. We tried several times for a peaceful resolution. Your father didn't take into consideration that we outnumbered him. If he hadn't shot my friend, he would be walking away with you. If you're going to survive, you will have to be smarter than that."

Neither the boy nor his mother said anything, they only turned and walked away. Jack went over to see how Paul was doing and Mark said he'd be fine. He was going to be in a lot of pain for a little while, but they needed to get him home. Paul had a little medical clinic in his house. It was much better than a first-aid kit and they can get him fixed up there. Jack had everyone unload the wagon, putting everything right on the ground. They carried it in after the carriage left with Paul. Jack's priority was to get Paul home as soon as possible.

Mark and Nikki left with Paul and the rest stayed behind. They got everything moved in and the window boarded up. Ralph took Josh's room and Brandon set up in the spare room. It would be the first time in months they slept on a bed. It would also be the first time in months they slept in separate rooms. Jack told Ralph he'd be back the next day or two to help them with windows. Everyone said their farewells and went their separate ways.

Julie and Prince

JOE, JULIE, AND THEIR SON PRINCE WALKED DOWN THE road and looked for places they could scavenge. They "escaped" the FEMA camp in Puyallup because it was getting too dangerous. They left at night, avoiding the roving patrol, and climbed the fence near the blue gate on Meridian Avenue. That was three nights ago, and they were out of food. Joe said they needed to get to Mount Rainier National Park, where they could take over a cabin or room in the hotel. They would need to walk about 50 miles and Joe thought it would take a week or so to get there. He also thought finding food would be easier than the reality they faced.

When they got to Graham, the small family turned off Meridian and onto the back streets to search for food and water. They scanned the houses looking for signs they may be empty. It was difficult to tell a lot of times with electricity being out. They came across a house with an empty driveway and all the curtains closed. They walked up to the front door and knocked. If anyone answered, he would ask for food and water. But nobody answered the door. They walked around to the back and Joe found a heavy rock and broke a window with it. They waited a few minutes to see if there would be a reaction from the inside. Still nobody came. Joe used the same rock to clear away the glass from the edges and lifted Prince inside. "Open the back door and let us in," Joe said.

When he looked around, Joe saw signs of life. Whoever lived here hadn't abandoned the house, they were just out.

Joe said, "We need to hurry. Take anything useful and let's be out of here in five minutes."

Julie went to the kitchen to look for food and found a box of MREs on the counter. She scooped up the box and set it by the back door, then went back to the kitchen. There were a few 1-gallon jugs of water on the counter as well. She uncapped the bottles for a sniff and taste test. It was water. She set those by the back door and went to tell Joe. He was in the bedroom and found a Ruger thirty-eight special in the nightstand. He felt like a wild-eyed country boy. A revolver wasn't his first choice, but beggars can't be choosers. From there he went to the closet to search for more ammunition and weapons. He found one box of ammo on the shelf in the closet. But that was the small find. On the floor of the closet was a full backpack. He picked it up and set it on the bed to look inside. This was somebody's bug out bag. The backpack contained spare clothes and survival gear. This was indeed a lucky day for the family.

Julie walked in and said, "I found MREs and water in the kitchen."

Joe said, "That's awesome. I found this," he showed her the revolver and continued, "and the backpack full of survival gear. Someone is looking out for us."

Julie said, "Find another bag for the MREs and let's get the heck out of here."

They searched around and found a smaller backpack and filled it with the MREs. Prince found a SOG survival knife in a sheath and said, "Can I keep it?"

Joe smiled at his son and said, "Of course you can."

Joe and Julie shouldered their packs, and each picked up a jug of water. They left out the back door and continued their march toward the park. They stayed in the back streets for a little while longer and eventually moved back to Meridian. They followed the road but stayed off the road. Anyone could see them coming from a long way off if they were on the road. It was also easier on the feet to stay off the pavement. They made good distance but didn't go as far as Joe thought they would with the packs weighing them down. They turned off Meridian when Joe saw the sign for Camp Arnold. That was a Salvation Army campground and Joe thought there might be food and water there. It was getting dark, so they made camp off-road and would check it out in the morning.

The next morning, they had an MRE and a little water for breakfast, then walked to Camp Arnold. Once again, they stayed off the road and walked through the trees. They didn't know if anyone was there and if there were people there, they didn't know if it would be safe. They skirted around the clearing to stay hidden. There were people at the camp, but Jack saw no one wearing uniforms. The Salvation Army owns the camp and they wear uniforms. That may have changed by now, but Joe didn't want to risk it. There were too many people there to fight off. Joe frowned and motioned for his family to follow him back to Meridian.

They would have to make their food and water last because

their next real shot at finding either was in Eatonville. There were a few homes between Camp Arnold and Eatonville, but Joe didn't count on any of them being empty. He had a gun, but homeowners also have guns, and he wasn't willing to risk it. They weren't that desperate yet, and he'd rather save the ammo for something he could eat.

They took two days to get to Eatonville from Camp Arnold. Prince slowed them down, and Julie thought he needed to rest. Joe said they would find a place in Eatonville, where they could rest a few days, but he didn't want to stay any longer. The closer to civilization they stayed, the more dangerous it would be. He wanted to be in the park to claim a spot as soon as possible. As they neared Eatonville, they saw more houses, but none looked approachable. He started to think Eatonville wasn't affected as much as the cities. True, they had no power or gasoline, but he couldn't find an abandoned home. People in the cities head for the hills, people in the hills stay put.

They followed Washington Avenue and made their way into town. All the stores were closed, so at least that much was "normal." Joe saw the high school and considered breaking into the kitchen but assumed it was empty by now. They walked down Washington for a few blocks, then turned onto Carter Street to see what they could find. As they walked, they noticed people staring at them through windows. *This will not be easy*, Joe thought. Julie broke the silence with the same conclusion and said, "None of these houses are empty and everyone is looking at us."

Joe said, "You're right on both counts. Just keep walking and try not to look suspicious. We'll turn down this next street and then go back to Washington Avenue. They made the turn and saw two men approaching. Joe took his wife's hand and she took Prince's hand. When they got close, one man held his hand up at the family, motioning for them to stop. Both of the men looked to be about 5'9" but the similarities stop there. The man that put his hand out had brown hair and a medium build. The other man had blonde hair that was almost white, and he was rail thin.

The bigger man said, "What are you up to?"

Joe said, "We've been walking since Puyallup and are making our way to Rainier. Our son is tired and we're looking for a place to rest for a day or two and refill our water jugs."

"You won't find any place to sleep here, these are our homes. You can try the park, or maybe the dugout at the high school. That would keep the wind off you, anyway. As for water, follow me. I've got a well. We won't let you die, but we will be watching you until you leave."

Julie said, "Thank you."

They walked a few blocks to the man's home and refilled the jugs, then walked up to the park. Julie asked if they could spare any food and the men said they'd see what they could come up with. Joe set up the survival tent for Prince and made a little fire to keep warm.

⌘

They stayed there for two days with the eyes of Eatonville on them the entire time. True to the big man's word, he didn't let them die. They scrounged up some food for the family and refilled their water bottles before they left. Their next big stop was in Elbe. It was a much smaller town, but as with Eatonville, they knew people were watching them. They sat at the bench at Scale Burgers to have some water and rest. Joe took off his pack and searched around for the food bars he knew were in there. He found two and gave one to Prince and shared the other with Julie.

Same as Eatonville, two men approached the family. As they got closer, Joe saw it was a man and a teenage boy. The man's jacket had a badge on it and Joe saw he was a national park ranger.

The Ranger said, "Hi, I'm John, and this is Brad. Where you headed?"

Joe said, "Seems to be everyone's first question."

Joe gave him the story and asked why John wasn't at the park.

John said, "I hate to break it to you, but the park isn't as safe as you may think. There are a lot of people there and you may not find a place to stay. All the Rangers left to be with their families and to escape the danger. I assume a lot of people have died since we left, so there may be a place to stay, but how will you survive?"

Joe said, "I've got a gun and some ammo. I plan to hunt for food just like everyone else is doing."

John said, "I wish you luck. Sorry I didn't have better news for you."

Joe said, "I hate to beg, but it's been a common theme on our trek from Puyallup. If you could spare any food or water, we would be grateful."

John said, "I can take your jugs and fill them for you. I'll ask my wife if we could spare any food."

Joe and Julie thanked John and rested at the bench and table. John and Brad returned about thirty minutes later with full water jugs, a jar of pickled cabbage, and some venison.

John said, "We don't have anything you could take on the road, but this should fill you up today."

Julie said, "Thank you very much. We appreciate it."

John and Brad walked away and the family ate. They rested for about an hour more, then shouldered their packs and left Elbe.

As they made their way toward the park, Joe was having second thoughts about staying there. The Rangers words were eating at him.

He said, "Maybe we should look for something outside the park. There must be some vacant hunting cabins all over the place. We should look for one instead."

Julie said, "That sounds better than what's waiting in the park. So let's try that first."

They weren't able to make Ashford before dark and found a spot off the road to make camp for the night. They made a few side trips along the way to look for empty cabins, so they didn't get as close to Ashford as Joe thought they would. Dinner was a few sips of water, they had to ration what food they had left and only ate their own food once a day. They always gave Prince extra, however. The family talked for a while before laying down to sleep.

When morning came, they packed up and made for Ashford. It took about an hour and a half to get there, and they couldn't believe how quiet it was. The businesses were boarded up and nothing moved. They scouted out the river-side of Ashford first, hoping to find a spot near the fresh, clean water. After a few hours of searching, they saw nothing promising and went back and crossed to the other side of town. They walked all day searching and found nothing.

Julie said, "If we don't find anything tomorrow, we should try our luck in the park."

Joe said, "Have a little faith. I'm sure we'll find something soon."

The next day they continued searching, and towards midday they thought they found something that would work. They found a small cabin without a vehicle in front. They watched the cabin for about an hour and didn't see any signs of life. Then they used the trees as cover and moved around to the back and waited again. Nobody saw anyone moving inside. They came out of the trees and walked around to the front and knocked on the door. Nobody answered.

Joe said, "You stay here and I'll get Prince through the back window. If you see anybody, shout."

Julie nodded her head. Father and son went around back. A few minutes later, Prince opened the front door. The family scooted inside and locked the door. Julie saw the pump for the well and her eyes lit up. She said, "We won't have to worry about water, that's a relief. We will have to do something about the window, however."

Joe said, "Don't worry about that. I'll figure out something."

They looked around and picked out their bedrooms. It thrilled them to know that sleep would come on real beds tonight. Joe said he would go out and try to find something to eat, and Julie got to work making the cabin a home. All Prince wanted to do was test out his new bed. He laid down and within five minutes the boy was sound asleep. A few hours later Joe returned with a dead bobcat.

Joe said, "Look what I got! I can't believe how big this thing is. I always thought bobcats were smaller. Get Prince's knife for me so I can clean this thing."

Prince ran out of his room with the knife and said, "Can I watch?"

Julie said, "We're going to eat a cat?" She shook her head and went into Prince's room.

Father looked to son and said, "Of course! You need to know how to do this."

They went outside but didn't go too far. It was already dark and Joe didn't want to get lost but, they also didn't want the guts too close to the cabin. They brought a lantern from the cabin with them so Joe could see what he was doing. Before long they finished cleaning the cat. Then Joe skinned it. The cat was ready for the fire. They went back to the cabin and Julie already had one going. They would all eat good tonight.

The next morning the family woke up and had a breakfast of bobcat. They discussed what they would do for the day. Joe said he wanted to scout around in the morning to get his bearings. He was also curious to know what was in the shed and would see about breaking in later in the day. Joe took his walk and came back a few hours later. He was home for about fifteen minutes when they heard something outside. He peeked out the window and saw a few armed men and heard a horse. Joe whispered to Julie and Prince, "Get in the room and hide."

Joe waited, crouched in the living room and faced the door. After a few agonizing minutes, he heard a man asking them to come out of the cabin. Then he heard a key turn the lock and the door opened. Joe fired and the man jumped back. Pain. He fell back and his vision blurred. His chest was on fire. People were coming in and he couldn't move. He whispered, "Sorry Julie."

Julie heard the gunshots and the hair on her arms stood up. She froze as if rooted to the floor. Then she heard men's voices and doors opening. It was then she realized her husband was dead, and she didn't know what to do. She told Prince, don't cry and don't speak. The door opened and she screamed, "Don't shoot!"

A man told her to come out of the room with her hands on her head. Julie went out first, followed by her son. They were escorted to the living room and questioned. The man she assumed was the leader said they would have to get their things and go. Julie shouldered the backpack with the survival gear and put the smaller one on Prince. She added a few blankets from the cabin, hoping the men wouldn't notice. Julie asked how to get to the park and the leader gave her directions.

They made it to Ashford and turned towards the park. They saw two people on bicycles turn off the road and jump off their bikes. Then they walked around behind the building. Julie saw the chance and didn't miss it. She said, "Run." They ran for the bikes and rode off as fast as they could. She never turned around to see if the cyclists saw them. After a few minutes, she slowed down and told Prince he could take it easy now. She couldn't believe their luck.

She said, "It's a new world we're living in, and if people are too stupid to protect what they have, then they lose it. Remember that."

Near sundown, they made it to the park entrance and Julie saw a few buildings off to the right. She thought, *this is a good place to camp out before going further*. She asked Prince for his knife and checked the buildings. They were small and old, and someone had already forced open the doors, but nobody was inside. She chose the cleanest one and tied the door shut was a paracord she found in the backpack. It wouldn't stop a determined person, but would keep the animals out and give them a warning if someone was trying to get in. The man wouldn't give the gun back, but at least they had the knife.

The next day they rode into the park. She had visited a few times in her life and knew there was a hotel with cabins not too far off. That was her destination, but before they got there, two armed men stop them. A man said, "Get off the bikes," and escorted them to Longmire. The men wouldn't talk so she didn't know if they were in danger or not. They passed the hotel and the men led them to a small office. The sign read: Ranger Station.

Second Man

A WEEK AFTER MOVING THE FAMILIES IN, JACK RECEIVED A message from Paul. Paul wanted Jack to spend the weekend with him to make sure Jack knew what to do should anything happen to him. He sent a message back telling Paul he would be there and try not to die too soon. He worried about leaving Diane alone all weekend, however. The first time he left her alone, she killed someone who tried to rape her. The second time, she took in a stranger. That turned out good, Robin was a good addition. She wasn't a member of the group yet but would be soon.

Today was Friday and Jack was getting prepared to leave. He only needed a change of clothes because Paul had everything else. He put the clothes in the day pack that carried his EDC items. He kissed Diane and said, "I'm leaving now and will be back Sunday. I'll get away sooner if I can." He winked and said, "Try to stay out of trouble this time, okay?"

Diane's eyebrows scrunched together, and she pursed her lips. She said, "That's getting old."

Jack put his hands up and said, "Ouch, sorry. I trust you to handle yourself just fine. I was only poking fun, won't happen again."

Now Diane smiled.

Diane watched Jack walk out the door and sat down with a book. After a few chapters, she decided she would go for a little hunt. The cottage was too quiet now. She needed to do something, so she grabbed her bow and quiver, strapped on her Glock, and walked out the door with both dogs. She still wouldn't go anywhere without one or two dogs, and they were great hunters. Hunting was a lot easier when she only had to follow the dogs. They went behind the cottage and made their way towards the park. After about twenty minutes Basha growled and was looking towards a big cedar tree.

Diane unholstered her Glock and said, "Whoever you are, you can stop hiding."

A tall skinny man walked out from behind the tree. His clothes were filthy, and he had a long, scraggly black beard. He had a handgun as well, but Diane didn't know what kind.

The man said, "You don't belong here."

Diane said, "I belong where I need to go. This is a National Park and anyone can be here."

"No ma'am, this is my property now and your trespassing."

"Look, it's a big park and there is plenty of game for both of us. So you go your way and I'll go mine, but I'm not leaving until I want to leave."

"Maybe, maybe not. But we'll see. We will see."

The man turned and ran into the bushes. Basha and Mercedes started to give chase, but Diane called them back.

She wondered what the man meant by "we will see." The man ran off to the north, so she headed east for about another thirty minutes before turning around and going home. Her hunt was eventful, but she came up empty. And she didn't shoot anybody.

Jack made it to Paul's and knocked on the front door. Paul usually had a sixth sense about people arriving and was outside waiting. Today was the first time he could remember knocking on the door. Michelle opened the door and invited Jack in, then got back to cleaning the enormous house. Paul was lying on a recliner, there was a tall glass of water on the end table next to him.

"Hello Jack," Paul said. "I'm sorry I didn't greet you, I was taking a little nap. The pain meds have that effect on me, but I'm hoping I took the last one today. I don't enjoy being reliant on medication."

Jack said, "If you're not ready, I can come back in a few days or next weekend."

"No no no, today is fine. You can't keep a good man down. Let's have a little lunch and we'll get started." Michelle came out with a tray of food and set it on the table. Lunch was vegetable soup, and elk steak, and a few potatoes. *I can get used to this*, Jack thought.

Out loud he said, "You've got quite the set up here."

Paul said, "Yes, I've done well for myself. As recent events have shown me, I'm not going to live forever and one day this will all be yours."

"I hope it's a long time from now. I'm very happy and

comfortable in my cottage. An address change can wait. Stick around."

"Well, I'm not planning on dying anytime soon. We're just preparing because anything can happen."

The men finished their lunch and Paul showed Jack to the communications room. It was the smallest room in the house, set in the back and on the second floor. The second floor got more light, so Paul wouldn't have to use any electricity to light the room most of the day. He always thought the satellite modem worked better higher up too. He showed Jack the set up and the radio to contact Ranger John. The radio and charger sat on a shelf with some spare equipment. The modem connected to a laptop on a plain brown desk with a comfortable black office chair. Jack thought it was strange with all the extravagance in this house, that this one desk looked like it came from IKEA. But he said nothing and listened to what Paul had to say. Next to the laptop was a notebook and a pen.

Paul said, "We don't use our names when we contact each other. It's only supposed to be for radios, but we adapted it to messages as well. You might find this surprising, but my call sign is Lumberjack." Jack laughed and Paul continued, "You will be Strider. Over in Morton, we call Jason Ice. Jim is an Eatonville and we call him Bourbon. He's an old man and doesn't get out of the house much anymore, so his number 2 does all the legwork. His name is Richard, and they never got to us with the call sign for him. I've been in contact with Jim a lot lately, so maybe I'll remember to ask about Richard's call sign. I'll let you in on a little secret, Sam and Josh took a while getting out of Puyallup and then got sidetracked in Eatonville. I'll fill you in on the whole story later."

Jack said, "You've heard from them? I assumed Josh died and

Sam decided to stay with the hospital, or he died too. Why haven't you told us?"

Paul said, "Sam was a prisoner at the hospital, courtesy of the National Guard. Josh helped him escape and the National Guard pursued them. They hid at Josh's hunting cabin in Eatonville and expect to be here in the spring. I didn't tell anyone because if the National Guard caught them, it would be a huge letdown for the group."

Jack said, "I see. That makes sense I guess."

Paul finished showing the ropes in the communication room and then went downstairs for formal introductions to the staff. He introduced Jack to Tabatha the cook, and formally introduced him to Michelle, the maid. He had seen them both before, of course. But they never talked much, so he didn't really know them. Then they went outside and talked to Tim and Angela, the security detail. They had just finished their lunch and were getting back to work. In all the times Jack had been Paul's house, he had never seen the couple. They moved on to the stables were Larry and Martha took care of the horses. Jack already knew Larry from the trip to Morton during the summer. He had met Martha too but didn't mind the formal introduction. Larry and Martha also raised the pigs and chickens.

From there Paul took Jack to the warehouse. This was no shed like everyone else had on their property. This was an actual warehouse, made of cement and rebar and was bigger than Paul's house. Jack thought it was 50 to 60 yards long and at least 30 yards wide. There were no windows and Jack knew the reason, the warehouse was also a fallout shelter. There were two filtered air vents in the ceiling. They walked inside and looked around. Wood filled a lot of the warehouse, most of it was for building cabins should they need to consolidate to one location. The location would be Paul's property. There were also enough poles and a large gate for the front of the property should the need arise. A large chain-link fence and barbed wire already surrounded the perimeter.

Jack saw pallets full of food pouches, candles, clothes, and other necessities. There were 50-gallon buckets marked beans, pasta, and rice. Stairs were leading to a raised section and Jack knew there were weapons and ammunition up there. Paul saw his eyes looking up there and said, "The fireworks section! I've added more stuff up there over the years, but it's still mostly fireworks."

Paul gave Jack the grand tour of the warehouse, showing him every nook and cranny. After the tour was over, they went back to the house for dinner and called it a day. Dinner was a salad, another elk steak, and more potatoes. Paul said, "We all eat good, but the variety is limited these days."

Jack said, "You'll never hear me complain. The food is delicious and you are good company."

Jack woke up at 7 AM the next day as usual. It didn't surprise him to see Paul already up and around. The shot to the arm didn't seem to slow him down at all.

Paul said, "Good morning, sleepyhead. Are you ready for some breakfast?"

Jack said, "I can smell the bacon. It's been months since I've had bacon. So yes, I am more than ready!"

They sat down at the table and had coffee while they waited for the food. About five minutes later Michelle brought out the tray and Jack's eyes watered. She set down his plate in his eyes locked on to the four thick strips of bacon. There were also a few eggs. Paul's plate had hash browns in addition to the bacon and eggs. Paul knew Jack long enough to know he would not eat the hash browns. Although, it occurred to him he should have asked. Jack ate the potatoes yesterday. But true to his word, Jack did not complain. He savored the smoky flavor of the bacon instead.

Paul said, "Now that your fed let's take a walk and work all that off."

Jack said, "Where are we going?"

Paul said, "We're going to walk the perimeter of the property so you know your way around."

They looked out the back door and turned left. Then they followed the fence line for about 200 yards before it forced them to turn right. They walked a few minutes and came to the stream crossing the property. It was about 5 feet wide, and Paul said it didn't go dry in the summer. It makes a great secondary source of water but doesn't have any fish. There was a fallen tree crossing the river Paul had used as a bridge until two years ago. The old tree had become too slippery, so Paul built a bridge to replace it.

Jack said, "Have you heard anything about our enemy? Like who they are and why they've been silent. I still think they're letting winter thin the herd and will hit us hard in the spring or summer."

Paul said, "You're probably right about thinning the herd. People will be scared, watching their friends and family die of disease, starvation, or cold. For the survivors, it will be traumatizing. They could be waiting just to let people terrorize themselves. As far as who they are, nobody knows yet. Everything is still just a guess."

Jack said, "As the president been heard from at all?"

"Not a peep."

They finished walking the perimeter and Paul showed him where the cabins would go should the need arise. There would be one cabin each for all the members. He showed Jack where the fields would go for farming. They would use the stream to help irrigate the farm. They walked back to the house and Paul said, "I think I've shown you everything, do you have any questions?"

Jack said, "Only one. If something does happen to you, how are we going to build all this? You are the only real carpenter if I'm not mistaken."

Paul said, "You are correct. I have the plans for all the cabins in my office, along with a diagram of the farm fields and what we should plant where, and at what times. I trust all of you can read the plans."

"I hope there are people better at it than I am. But I hope more that you stick around, and we don't need to worry about it."

Paul laughed and shook his head.

They walked inside and Jack said, "If there's nothing else, I'd like to get home. Diane is by herself and I worry."

Paul said, "Tabatha has prepared a special meal for you, she would be disappointed if you didn't eat it."

Jack said, "I would hate to disappoint Tabatha."

Her special meal was an elk meatloaf wrapped in bacon. There was a salad, a side of green beans, and more potatoes.

Jack said, "You need to stop showing me how wonderful the cook is or I may decide to move in early!"

Paul laughed and said, "I'll tell Tabatha you love the meal."

"Yes, absolutely. It was delicious."

After they finished lunch, Jack stood to leave and Paul stopped him.

"I have a little gift for you before you leave." He yelled, "Michelle, bring the package!"

Michelle brought in something wrapped in paper and handed it to Paul. Paul handed it to Jack and said, "Have some more bacon."

Jack smiled and said, "You are a great man, Paul Peterson."

Paul walked Jack outside, and they said their farewells. Jack thanked Paul for the wonderful food and the parting gift and started for home.

The Hunter

DIANE WOKE UP THE NEXT MORNING AND MADE HERSELF some breakfast. It felt strange waking up alone. She didn't mind, but it made her feel a little empty. When breakfast was finished, she took the dogs for a short walk. On most days the dogs were walked first, but she was starving today and didn't understand it. Then she remembered she missed her last cycle in her mouth went dry. *No... no, it can't be*, she thought. She whisked that thought out of her mind and thought of something else instead... anything but that.

Diane got home and cleaned up after breakfast then sat down on the couch. But she couldn't get that thought out of her head and went hunting again. The walking and searching kept her focused. She grabbed her bow and quiver and walked out the door with the dogs. Once again, she headed for the park, because the hunting was better than outside the park. She let the dogs lead because they were hunting dogs, after all. Jack used them for ducks, pheasants, and other birds. But he said they would hunt anything you asked them to. He gave them deer scent after Brandon took down the first one. He said it was a risk because the dogs may stop hunting for everything else because they go crazy over deer scent. It was a risk he needed to take, however.

Birds were fine, and there was grouse in the area, but there weren't enough to survive on. They needed the ability to find everything in the area that was edible: deer, elk, birds, rabbits, cougar, and various other animals. The moose were safe because Jack thought moose meat was disgusting. It was rare to see one, anyway. The dogs have been good so far and if they ever concentrated on only deer, Jack hoped he could retrain them on others. As a breed, German Wirehairs are smart. Basha and Mercedes do not disappoint.

After about thirty minutes Diane heard something behind her. The dogs notice too. Diane scanned the trees looking for game, but the dogs gave a low growl. Diane lowered her bow and pulled out her Glock. She said, "Basha go." Basha ran straight for the tree and sat down on the other side of it. Diane said, "You can stop hiding. We know you're there."

A man stepped out from behind the tree, choosing the side opposite of the dog. He was a tall man and had his hands up as he stepped out. She saw a rifle slung over his shoulder and a handgun on his hip. Diane said, "Don't move." The man nodded his head.

Diane asked, "Why are you following me?"

He said, "You're on my land and you need to turn around and go home."

Diane shook her head and said, "This is a National Park. Neither of us owns it and both of us can hunt here. There are plenty of animals for both of us."

The man looked down on her with a stern face and said,

"Laws don't apply anymore. The Rangers left. As far as I'm concerned, they gave up the park when they left. This is my park now. So turn yourself around and go home, I'd hate to see anything happen to that pretty little face."

She saw the blinding light in her head again and she heard the words, "I'll be gentle." She looked center mass. Tunnel vision so acute she could almost see his heart pumping. But she didn't fire this time. Something was holding her back and she couldn't figure it out. Then she remembered Jack's words last summer in Elbe. *He may not be alone.* She took several deep breaths and came back to herself.

Diane said, "We were first, but we're not stingy. We're willing to share the game."

The man said, "We are not. You go back and tell your husband and friends this area is off limits. If we see you here again, you won't get the chance to tell anybody anything."

As he finished his last words, his friends appeared out of the woods. The four men were hanging back about 20 yards. Diane realized Jack just saved her life, and he wasn't even here. Her instinct was to kill the man and had she done so, his friends would surely have returned fire. It concerned her that the man knew about Jack, Ralph, and Brandon. She had said "we" to make the man think she was not alone in the woods. Now she wondered how much more the man knew about her. Unable to out-gun the small group, Diane had no choice but to return home.

She got home but didn't go inside, she still needed to find some game. When she got to the cabin, she turned north and back into the woods. She hadn't gone this way too many times, but she hunted this area enough she wouldn't get lost. She did not want to go home empty-handed. She needed to prove to Jack that she was fine on her own and wouldn't kill people on a whim. Bringing home dinner would be the icing on the cake.

Diane walked for about an hour and the dogs weren't giving any clues about nearby game. It was harder outside the park because there were a lot of cabins and homes back here. "A lot," is relative to a small, small town. Just as she was about to turn back, she caught movement out of the corner of her eye. She looked at the dogs and their little tails were wagging, meaning they were on scent. She didn't want the dogs to run up and chase whatever it was away, so she whispered, "Sit." Both dogs parked their rumps on the ground, but their heads turned towards the animal. Their faces were shaking with excitement. It took all their self-control to sit there and wait.

Diane knocked an arrow and concentrated where she'd seen the movement and where the dogs were looking. She took a few steps forward, trying to get a better look. The deer lifted her head and Diane saw it. She raised the bow and drew. It was an easy 20-yard shot. But the deer caught her movement and ran just after Diane fired. She hit the deer but not where she wanted and not a kill shot. Diane said, "Basha, Mercedes, go!" The dogs took off in a flash and chased the deer through the forest. The deer was injured and bleeding, so the dogs had no trouble chasing her down. It was over in about 30 to 45 seconds. The dogs brought the deer down and Mercedes bit down on the neck and shook her head violently. She finished what Diane started.

Diane caught up to the dogs and told them what good girls they were and made sure to pet them and thank them. Then she pulled out her knife and field dressed the animal so she would be easier to drag home. She was not looking forward to dragging that deer all the way home by herself, especially when this one didn't have antlers to hold onto. She would have to drag the deer by the front legs to avoid the scent glands on the back legs. After a while of hard dragging, she realized the deer was small enough to sling over her shoulders. She wore the deer like a cape and made better time. It was still slow going, however, and she took almost 2 hours to get home.

Intelligence

JACK RETURNED HOME AND WAS A LITTLE SURPRISED HE didn't see an extra car in the driveway. Now if there weren't any dead bodies lying around, he would consider it a success. When he got closer, he saw the deer hanging from a tree and thought, *that's my girl!* He yelled, "Nice shot!" As expected, the door flung open and two very excited dogs came running at him. With just two words he could complement Diane, get the door open without fiddling for his keys, and hug his dogs.

Jack said, "I'm glad there are no new cars in the driveway and the only dead body is one we can eat. It is the only dead body, right?"

Diane said, "I told you the jokes are getting old."

She slammed the door shut, leaving Jack and the dogs outside.

Jack always thought Diane could take a joke. Then he thought maybe the new normal was getting to her and he would have to think before he opened his mouth. He opened the door and went inside to apologize. He promised her he'd knock it off and try to be more careful.

Diane said, "I don't know why but it's just irritating. I'll have you know, I could have shot someone today but held back. I remembered your wise words in Elbe, about waiting to see their true numbers. I was talking to one man, but four others were hiding. They told me we weren't allowed to hunt in the park, and they know about you, Ralph, and Brandon. I don't know how long they've been watching us but, it's a little creepy."

Jack said, "This is troubling. I'm going to have to get with Paul and decide a course of action."

"We need to chase them down as soon as possible. I offered to share the hunting, and they declined. They aren't open to reason. I wanted to shoot the smug off his face and tell his friends we had a much bigger group. But I let him live and kept my mouth shut. Of course, had I killed him, I would be dead and not talking to you now."

"We'll go see Paul tomorrow. We can't go chasing them without knowing anything about them. As long as they think it's just the four of us, they won't think we're too much of a threat. We have time to get some intelligence on them then make a plan. Today, we need to inventory our guns and ammo. Then we can rest."

Diane said, "Inventory? That sounds like a load of fun."

Jack said, "Yes. That includes the safe room. I need to see you open it successfully so you will be responsible for the safe room."

Diane rolled her eyes and went to the bedroom to unlock the

room. She remembered everything and was soon down below taking inventory.

The next morning, Jack walked the dogs while Diane cooked. They had steak, eggs, and bacon for breakfast. Diane almost cried when she had her first by the bacon in months.

Jack said, "It's good to know the boss." They both laughed.

They cleaned up the breakfast mess and made their way to Paul's house. Jack sent Paul a message with a summary of what happened before he went to bed last night. He let Paul know they would be there after breakfast. The dogs came with them this time.

When they arrived, Paul was waiting for them in the driveway. They said their hellos and went inside. Then Diane gave Paul a full rundown of what happened the day before. Paul raised eyebrows a few times but kept quiet as she told the story. When she finished, he said, "This is worrisome. Give me a minute, I'll contact Jason and Brett and tell them to get here ASAP.

Paul went upstairs to the communication room and fired off a quick message to the two men.

I need you to get to my house as soon as possible — pack for an overnight trip to the park. You will be scouting and will have a partner.

You'll be gone for two nights.

~ Paul

He went back downstairs to rejoin his guests. They discussed a plan and wondered who could be taking the lead with the park survivors.

Jack said, "I thought most the people in the park would be dead by now. I hear occasional gunfire coming from that direction, so I knew somebody was alive in the park. I did not think they had banded together, however."

Paul said, "We'll let Jason and Brett gather the intelligence. Then we'll see if we can strike up a bargain. I'd like to make allies instead of enemies. It's always better to have friends. In the meantime, I want everyone to stay out of the park."

They discussed a few strategies, but it was a waste of time without knowing who they were dealing with or how many of them there were. Jack offered to wait until they ran out of ammo. And then we can walk in and take over. But Paul nixed that idea saying they couldn't afford to wait that long, a lot of us may starve before then. So, they passed the time trading stories, and Paul transferred some of his wisdom to Diane. Within a few hours, Jason and Brett showed up and were filled in on the situation.

Jason said, "So we just go in, see what they got, and get out?"

Paul said, "That's exactly what we need. Avoid contact. Once we have a bigger view of the situation, we can figure out what to do."

Brett said, "So we should get going."

Paul said, "Hold your horses, and I mean that. You don't need to walk all that way when I have horses. Each of you take a horse and ride to the park entrance. Jack and Diane can then lead your horses back to their house and pick you up the next day."

Jack said, "That sounds like a great plan, but it's getting late in the day. I think we should ride to my cottage first. Jason and Brett can crash there, and we can get started in the morning. Are you okay with that, Diane?"

Diane said, "Of course, no problem. They can get a taste of that fine young doe I took down yesterday. With the help of Basha and Mercedes."

Paul said, "Great, it's a plan. I'll get Larry and Martha to saddle up four horses, and you can get on your way."

Paul went outside to get with Larry and Martha about the horses. Diane described the man she talked to in the park. Because he said it was "his" park, she thought he might be the leader. They agreed it was probably him, so Jason and Brett would be on the lookout for him. Diane laughed and said, "If You Get a Clean Shot, maybe take it."

Jason laughed and said, "Paul said to avoid contact, so we will. Besides, shooting him would make it very hard to get out of the park alive."

Diane said, "I understand. I don't want you to get shot or die, it was just a fantasy. He looked at me like I was beneath him."

Paul called them all outside to wait for their horses. Larry and Martha brought out the first two, saying they were for Jack and Diane. Larry said, "This is Missy. Brett will get her daughter Jeannine. As you know, Jeannine will follow her mother anywhere. So, it will make leading the horses home and back to the park much easier." A few minutes later they returned with two more horses, and everyone mounted up. Paul wished them luck and said, "Remember, no contact." Jason and Brett nodded their heads, and the group turned their horses towards Jack's cottage.

They made it to the cottage in good time with the horses, but it was still too late to move on to the park. They tied the horses up, and Jack took Jason to the shed to get the deer.

Jack said, "In all the years I've known you, I've never seen you butcher an animal. If you don't mind, I'd like to watch you and see if I can pick up a few tricks."

Jason said, "No problem, it would be my pleasure. Besides, what's the point of being a master of something if you can't teach others."

They went inside and put the deer on the counter. Jack retrieved a few good knives and a hatchet.

Jack said, "I don't want to rush you, but just know that this is dinner. Unless you have a set order, carve up four steaks and I'll throw them on the fire."

Jason said, "There is an order, but I'll see what I can do."

Jason put on a little class, and the other three occupants paid close attention to what he was doing. He carved out four steaks earlier in the process, then went back to his normal routine. Jack added a few herbs and got them cooking. Just before the steaks finished cooking, Diane prepared a few vegetables. They took a break to eat the food while it was hot, then resumed the class. When they finished, Jack chose a few good bones and tossed them at the dogs. They wrapped the meat in butcher paper, courtesy of Paul, and stored it in the shed.

Jack took the dogs outside, pointed at the horses, and said, "Guard." Then he offered Jason the couch to sleep on because he was too big for the couch bed in the other room. And he took Brett into the room and rolled the bed out from the couch for him. Jack said, "I wish I had better accommodations, but it could be worse. You could be on the couch."

The men laughed, and Jason said, "I heard that." And they laughed a little longer. Jack wished the men a good night, and they all went off to bed.

For breakfast the next morning, Jack shared some of Paul's bacon. Diane also prepared some venison and eggs.

Brett said, "I can't believe Paul held out on us like that. When I see him, I'm going to lay a serious guilt trip on him. I haven't had bacon since this mess started."

Jack said, "I'm sure if you asked nicely to fix you up."

Jason said, "I'm asking first!"

Jack grabbed two more bones out of the shed and thanked his dogs for watching the horses. He put them in the cottage with the bones and said he'd be back in no time. Then the small group mounted up and left for the park. Nothing had changed in Ashford proper since the last time Jack had been through. Except maybe it looked eerier in the dead of winter. Jack spurred his horse to get them out of the town faster. When they got to the park entrance, Jason and Brett dismounted and agreed upon a time to meet up the next day. Then they said their farewells. Soon the two men turned off the road and melted into the trees.

Longmire

THE MEN TOOK JULIE AND HER SON INTO THE RANGER station, but the small office was devoid of rangers. She saw a large man in his upper 50s with gray hair and a gray mustache. He was sitting and did not stand up so she could be for sure, but she figured him to be around 6'2" tall. The desk could not hide his enormous belly. He did not look up until one of the men spoke.

He said, "General, we found these two riding bikes up the road. We confiscated the bikes, what should we do with these two?"

The general said, "Leave them here. I'll see if they can do anything and make a decision."

The two men left the office and went back on their patrol, this time riding bikes.

The general looked Julie up and down, and she felt like she was on an auction block. She did not like the way the man was looking at her, the hair on her arms and neck was standing up, and she shivered. After what felt like hours, but was probably only a minute or two, he set his enormous frame back in the chair.

The general said, "Pvt. Rafino, get us some coffee."

Private said, "Yes, sir." He left the office to get the coffee.

The general said, "So, what are your talents?"

He raised his eyebrows when he said "talents" and Julie thought he looked creepy.

She did her best to remain calm and said, "I can cook."

"Not good enough. We have cooks, you're going to have to do better than that if you want a place to stay and food to eat."

She said, "I can sew. Repairing clothes is a useful talent now. You're not going to Walmart tomorrow to buy new clothes."

The general just stared at her and said nothing.

She continued, "I'm a healer."

The general gave a quick snort and said, "A doctor?"

"No."

"Nurse?"

"No, a naturalist."

The general gave a heavy sigh and shook his head in slow motion.

Julie said, "So you have a pharmacy then? Do you have a doctor or nurse? Can you treat a cold without medicine? How about headaches? You need me."

The general nodded but kept his face a mask. He needed a doctor, but he would try her out and see what happens. The door opened, and the private returned with the coffee as the general said he would give her a tryout as a healer. He told Pvt. Rafino to escort her and her son to their room. He said, "Yes, sir" and showed them out the door.

When they were out of earshot of the Ranger station, Pvt. Rafino said, "Don't mind him, he was never in the military and only tries to act cool. I don't know how they chose him as a leader."

When he said that, Julie raised her eyebrows and tilted her head and said, "You aren't with them? He called you private." This little bit of Intel intrigued her, and she wanted to keep Rafino talking. The more she knew, the more she could increase her chances of making it.

Pvt. Rafino pointed at the building and said, "Those are the working girls. That's where he wanted to send you. If you don't perform your job adequately, it's where you'll end up."

She shivered and said to herself, *Oh no. Not again. Never.*

She said aloud, "Why did he call you private if you're not with them?"

He said, "After the Rangers left, I took charge of this area. We were doing good and making our way. Then these jokers came out of the woods with their guns and claimed the area for themselves. We couldn't fight them because they were well armed, and we only had a few people with guns. They told us anyone with skills could stay, and they would escort all freeloaders out of the park.

He told her to stop talking until they got to her room, or someone might overhear them. They entered the hotel, and he got a key from behind the desk and showed her the way. He opened the door and gave her the key, then stepped aside to let her in. Julie and her son walked inside and looked around. There was a beautiful queen-size bed with a log frame and a dresser and nightstands to match. She was grateful he put her on the second floor so nobody could peek in, or worse. There was a washbasin in the corner with a mirror above.

She waved the private inside and asked him to continue his story. She said, "What did they do with the freeloaders?"

He said, "I don't think anyone was freeloading. But anyone who didn't have skills they wanted were escorted out. They never came back."

Julie said, "What happened after that? How did you become their private?"

He said, "I'm their private so that they can humiliate me. I told them I was a supervisor before the attacks, but didn't say where because I took them for anti-government types. So they told me I could supervise the hotel, but mostly I'm in the office with the general to do his bidding."

Julie said, "What about the working girls? I'm sure they didn't volunteer for that."

The private said, "Oh no. We all started off with different jobs, and everything was going fine. Then the men picked on a few of the girls and told them they weren't doing enough to earn their keep. After a few weeks of hounding them and threatening them with expulsion, the general gave them a choice... as if it was really a choice. He told the women they can provide comfort, or they could leave. Since leaving meant certain death, they 'chose' to stay."

Julie said, "Oh my, that's horrible."

"It is, and it will be your choice soon enough if you don't do your job, or the general decides he wants you anyway."

She said, "That fat oaf will not put a finger on me. I'll choose to leave." *Never again*, she thought.

"Be careful around him, these guys do whatever he says. I don't think any of them were in the military. In the military, you can refuse an unlawful order. I overheard a few of the guys saying the general was a high school janitor before all this went down."

Julie sat on a chair and said, "That makes perfect sense. I can always tell when someone has never been in a management position before. They're drunk with power."

Private Rafino said, "I need to get back before the general misses me."

The private left and Julie unpacked their meager belongings and put them in the dresser. She kept all the survival gear in the backpack because there was nowhere to put it all. It would also be easier packing up if they had to go. She would live at the park entrance if she had to. That general would not touch her. She got settled in and took a seat, then there was a knock at the door. Her son looked at her, and she said, "No, I'll get it."

She opened the door, and the man standing there was slightly out of breath.

He said, "It's time to prove your worth. Get to the general's office as fast as you can."

She picked up her backpack with the first aid kit inside and she ran out the door. She told her son to stay inside and locked the door behind her. Then she ran back to the general's office. When she got inside, she saw a man lying on the couch with other men surrounding him. She got in closer and saw a bloodied up shirt over his belly, and saw his face was pale white. She had a first aid kit, but they didn't know that, and she wanted to keep what she had. She asked them if they had a first aid kit. A few seconds later someone handed one to her.

She asked what happened and someone told her a cougar attacked him. She cut the man's shirt away and cleaned the wound with dry gauze. She asked for hot water and a clean rag. A man behind her said it was already coming. Someone had the forethought to apply pressure to the wounds, and the bleeding had stopped mostly by the time she got there. That told her the cuts probably weren't very deep, but he had still lost a lot of blood. The hot water and rag arrived, then she washed away the blood and dirt and got a better look at the wound. There were four cuts, but only one was deep enough where she considered stitching it up.

She asked if anyone had a needle and thread for stitching wounds. A man handed her a box, and she opened it to reveal a suture kit. She said, "This is going to hurt," then she began to stitch the wound closed. As she was closing him up, she asked someone to go to the hotel restaurant and see if they had any honey. A few minutes later someone ran in with a small jar half full of honey. She dripped honey over the wound and told them it was a natural antibiotic. Then she covered it with gauze and taped it down.

Julie said, "If you have any chemical antibiotics, it will help a lot. His biggest worry right now is an infection. If you can scrounge up some zinc, give him that too. How did you guys run into a cougar?"

Sgt. Morrison said, "We were scouting around Ashford and doing some hunting. On our way back the cougar pounced. Everybody around us is hunting for food now, and we must be putting pressure on the cougars. We are eating the same food, so now we are food. Of course, so is the cougar. He did not survive the fight."

The general said, "Did anything else happen?"

Sgt. Morrison said, "No. We told the redheaded woman to stay out of the park but didn't see her husband and friends. I'm sure she'll give them the message."

The general said, "Good. That will do for now. Eventually, we may have to raid them."

Julie said, "Don't move him or the wound may reopen. I'll be back in a few hours to check on him."

The Scout

JASON AND BRETT MOVED OFF THE ROAD TO THE LEFT. They kept about five yards to the side so they could see the road without being seen. The Nisqually River was on the right side and could cause problems. The river flooded some years back and washed out a campground just up the road. It was so long ago, neither Jason nor Brett could remember the name of the campground. So, for now it was best to stay to the left side. They moved slow to avoid making noise but still made steady progress.

There were a few times they had to leave the woods and get back on the road to avoid obstacles. They came upon Tahoma Creek and stopped. They couldn't cross the creek on foot because the water was too high, and they would get soaked. Their only choice was to walk across the bridge, which would leave them open for anyone watching to see them.

Jason said, "At least it's a short bridge and we can be across it in a hurry. "Let's watch for a few minutes and see if anything moves."

Brett said, "This isn't the bridge I would watch, so I think we're going to be okay. But yeah, let's watch."

The two men scanned the other side for about five minutes before they agreed it was probably safe to go. As they got to the tree line, they stopped and looked up and down the creek bed to make sure no one was down there. The fishing was probably good. Then they hurried across the bridge and melted back into the trees.

Some ways up the road there was another short bridge right off a bend in the road. They watched from the trees and determined it was clear, then made their way across again. Just a few hundred yards from that bridge was the third one, and it would be the most difficult. The bridge itself wasn't too long, but the crossing was.

Still in the trees, the two men stopped and looked. They could see a fair distance when they moved to the tree line and didn't notice anything.

Brett said, "Now this is the bridge I would watch. It's the closest one to Longmire and has a good view of anything coming their way."

Jason said, "I agree. I don't like it. Follow me."

Jason went back into the woods and took a path up the creek, then turned right towards the creek and walked up to the water.

Jason said, "There. We can cross that log and be on our way without getting seen."

They made their way to the log and got a closer look. It was smaller up close, but they figured it would do. It only needed to hold their weight. The log was dry, so the chances of them slipping were minimal. Jason went first and sidestepped his way across with ease. Jason was a hunting guide before the attack and had spent his life in the woods. That little log was just another day at the office. Brett was a reporter and didn't have that advantage. He got out and hunted when he could but was nowhere near as good as Jason. He took note of Jason's tactic and mimicked it as best he could.

He sidestepped his way across and made it about halfway before he lost his balance for an instant.

Brett said, "Oh crap! Next time tell me about the slippery spot."

Jason laughed and said, "Be quiet or taken this route won't make a difference. Besides, there was no slippery spot. You lack talent." Jason was still smiling.

Brett said, "If I wasn't hovering over ice cold water, I might have time to laugh."

Brett finally made it across and Jason said, "You took twice as long as me." Brett just shook his head because there was nothing he could say. That bridge marked the halfway point to Longmire, so Jason asked Brett if he needed a rest. Brett declined and said, "I'm not a slug. I may not have been born to the outdoors, but I'm in pretty good shape. I'll be fine." Jason nodded and they continued their hike.

Soon enough the two men approached Longmire. Right after the bend in the road, several cars were parked side-by-side, making an effective roadblock. There was a few feet of room on the Riverside of the road to let people get past. A horse would probably make it too. They decided to scout the south side first so they can be at the north side before it got dark. They would make camp on the north side so getting there before dark would make things easier. They stuck to the trees and watched from behind the parking lot. They saw more people than they thought they would, but very few had weapons. Anyone who had a weapon was a man. The few women they saw were all unarmed.

They knew the inn would be a hotspot of activity, and it gave them a good impression of how many armed men they would have to deal with. After about an hour of watching the inn, they moved to the admin buildings along the river. They could only see a few without getting caught, but didn't see any activity there. Jason figured the rest of the buildings were not in use either. From there they backtracked to the road-block and crossed the street. They would take the trail of shadows to cross in front of the inn without being seen. It's a small hike that would take them about ten minutes and possibly save their lives. The purpose of the small trail is to see the hot springs. It was very convenient for Jason and Brett.

Once on the other side, they hung out about 50 yards behind the ranger station. From there they saw a lot more activity, mostly armed men going back and forth. A few times they saw a red-haired lady that looked familiar. They didn't say anything, but looked at each other when they saw her. It confirmed to each of them that she was who they thought she was. They saw two men arrive on bicycles and a few minutes later two different men rode off on the bicycles. *Changing of the guard*, Jason thought. He noted the time and would check back every hour until he saw the next change. Knowing the time of a shift change would be huge.

Before it got too dark, they move towards the river to get a look at the other side of the admin buildings. Again, there was no activity that they could see. Cabins and trees obstructed their view, however. There is no way to get close enough without being seen. With nothing to see there, the two men returned to a spot behind the ranger station. Jason checked his watch and was happy to see they weren't going to miss a possible change of the guard.

It was dark now, and for once Jason was glad the electricity was off. His night vision was much better with no lights interfering. The same could be said for the people he was watching, however. They still had to keep their distance and stay hidden. The activity at the ranger station slowed down considerably after dark. They can see candlelight coming from the rooms in the inn. Jason assumed people were getting ready to go to bed. He or Brett would have to do the same.

Jason got close to Brett's ear and whispered, "I'll take first watch. I want to see the guard change."

Brett nodded and unrolled his sleeping bag and foam pad. Then he climbed inside and went to sleep. Those were the only words either of the men spoke aloud since arriving at Longmire. They could not risk being heard and caught. With no other background noise out in the forest, voices carry a long distance. Especially at night. At midnight, Jason finally saw what he wanted to see. Two men arrived on bicycles and two more men rode away with them the bikes. *Midnight, 8 AM, and 4 PM*, Jason thought. If it turns out the group needs to attack Longmire, they know the exact times they can move in without risk of being seen by the guards. Furthermore, all the guards will be at Longmire so there would be no stragglers seeking revenge.

A few minutes after the night shift rode away, two men walked behind the ranger station. Jason assumed it was the guards coming off shift. They were coming straight towards Jason and Brett. Jason shifted behind the large cedar tree he had been peering around. He hoped Brett didn't choose now to roll over in his sleep. He could hear the two men talking.

The first man said, "I think I might visit the house before going to bed."

The second man said, "Have fun, that's not my thing."

The first man said, "What, are you a prude?"

"No, I prefer a woman who isn't forced to be with me is all. I'd also prefer to be married first."

"Your loss."

The first man laughed, and Jason heard zippers unzipping. The men didn't say anything while they were relieving themselves, and Jason hoped they would turn around when they finish their business. They were close enough that Jason worried they would hit Brett and wake him up. But luck was on Brett's side, and he stayed dry. The two guards finished watering the plants and walked away saying goodnight to each other.

Jason gave it five minutes to be sure they were long gone before he woke Brett to take over the watch. He made his bed farther away to be sure he wouldn't sleep in urine or have to smell it. Brett's watch was uneventful until about six in the morning. He saw people leaving the inn to relieve themselves and go back in. Soon after he could smell food cooking and wished he was there. At 7 AM he woke Jason. Jason could smell the breakfast and was a little dismayed because all he had was a cold MRE. He reminded himself to ask Paul for some of that bacon. That would be a nice reward.

As expected, at 8 AM the bicycles returned and the guards changed. Jason now had an eight-hour shift confirmed. An hour later, they watched a large fat man in his upper 50s approach the ranger station and go inside. An unarmed brown-haired man ran up behind him yelling, "General! General! I have a message for you!" He went inside the ranger station so whatever the message was, went unheard by Jason and Brett. But they now had a very good description of the leader, or the presumed leader. They stayed for another hour and decided they'd seen what they needed to see. They could take their time and still be at the front gate before Jack and Diane. They followed the trail of shadows around to the other side and made their way to the roadblock and started for home.

They left the same way they came, following the road but in the trees for cover. They crossed the log again, and this time Brett had an easier go with it. For the next two bridges they used the same strategy as the day before, and made the crossings without issue. As they got near the park entrance, Jason thought they were safe and moved onto the road. A few seconds later, a shot ring out and Brett fell. Jason spun around and hit the ground. He saw two men with bicycles. One man aimed a rifle. Jason rolled towards Brett just before the rifle fired again.

He stood and grabbed Brett's arms and dragged him toward the trees. The man fired again. Jason took around in his side. He struggled but got them both behind the trees before another shot rang out.

Private Rafino ran to the office and yelled, "General! General! I have a message for you!" He followed the general inside and waited for the big man to get seated before handing him a slip of paper.

"One of the night guards handed it off to me and said it was important. Something about an old leader."

The general's eyes lit up at those words and he snapped, "Get out!"

Rafino left in a hurry and the general read the message:

I've been watching you and you have a nice little setup there. You look comfortable and well-fed while I'm out on my own. I hope you haven't forgotten about me, "General." You will have to pay the piper.

-I'm coming for you

The general eased his heavy load back into the chair and stared at the ceiling. He remembered how he took over as the leader.

The former leader, Dale Roberts, was an effective leader but I didn't care. I wanted to lead us through this mess. Dale didn't have what it took to be ruthless to those who aren't with us. He wanted to be nice to people and help them.

It was an easy coup. I only had to convince the others that we had to fight for ourselves if we were going to survive. Deep down, everyone is selfish. I only need to bring it to the surface. It was child's play.

I should have let Dale stay with us, but he took the role change bad so I sent him packing. Maybe I should have ended him instead. This is what I get for being nice.

The door opened and slammed shut, bringing general back to

the present. "Good morning, Colonel." He handed the colonel the note and waited for his response.

"What do you think, general?"

"I think he's just one man."

Jack heard the shot and looked at Diane. She nodded and said, "Go!" Jack spurred his horse and ran through the park entrance. Diane grabbed the reins of Missy and spurred her horse, but not as hard. She knew Jeannine would follow, but she was unsure about the horse she was holding. Jack rode as fast as he could, and a few hundred yards past the entrance he saw two men on bicycles. When they saw him, they turned around and rode the other way. Jack couldn't see his friends and was worried. He yelled, "Jason! Brett!"

He heard Jason yell, "Over here, need help!"

Jack jumped off his horse and saw Diane was close enough behind where he could leave the horse there. He ran towards Jason's voice and was shocked by what he saw. Brett was shot in the back and Jason was bleeding from the side.

Jason said, "I'll be fine, but Brett is in bad shape. He needs help fast."

Jack said, "Can you help me get him up?"

"I think so."

Jack helped Jason up and they got Brett to the road. Jason had already started first-aid by stuffing gauze in the hole. He knew it wasn't enough, but it was all he could do. They slung Brett over the saddle belly down, and tied his hands and feet to the stirrups with paracord. They rode off to Jack's cottage as fast as they could, but not as fast as they could go. The ride on the horse was bad for Brett, but they had no choice. Riding at full speed would be much worse.

When they got to the cottage, Jack ran inside and grabbed the keys to his truck. At the same time, Diane and Jason untied Brett. Jack flew out of the house and unlocked the tailgate. With Diane's help, he got Brett laid out on the bed of the truck. Jason joined him and would help keep him steady. Jack told Diane, "Contact Paul and tell him what happened. We need Mark there ASAP and will be there soon. Take care of the horses, Basha and Mercedes can help.

Jack climbed in the truck and headed for the gate. He jumped, out unlocked it, and took off without worrying about re-locking it. He sped straight for Paul's house. He opted for Paul over Mark's cabin. Paul was not only closer, but had an advanced medical room. A lot of doctors would be proud to call his little room their office. It even had a table for performing surgery. All that was missing was a doctor. Jack hoped it was enough.

Jack pulled in the driveway and saw Paul and Larry waiting for them. He didn't stop, however. He drove over the grass and right up to the house. Then he jumped out and pointed toward the tailgate and said, "In there." They got the tailgate open then Jack pulled Brett out. Paul and Jack picked him up and carried him to the medical room. Larry helped Jason inside.

When they got to the room, Jack saw Mark was not there yet. He said, "I'm well-trained and first-aid, but it won't be enough to save him. How long until Mark gets here?"

Paul said, "Hopefully within ten minutes. He is white as a

ghost, he must've lost a lot of blood. Unfortunately, that's one thing I could not stock up on."

Jack said, "Help me get his shirt off and we can try to stop the bleeding. We can get it cleaned up and ready for when Mark gets here. We need to do the same with Jason."

Jason said, "Don't worry about me, concentrate on Brett. It was my fault."

Paul said, "I don't want to hear anything about that right now. Now we concentrate on healing, so get your shirt off and let us clean you up and stop the bleeding."

Jason nodded and did as Paul instructed. As Paul cleaned him up, they heard more vehicles outside. Everyone looked at each other with the same confused look.

Jack said, "Did Mark drive here?"

Paul said, "I don't think so. He didn't say he would. I've got to run out and check. I have an idea who it could be."

Paul ran outside to see what was going on. When he saw Sam, his heart filled with joy and he said, "Thank God! You have perfect timing, scrub up!"

It wasn't the reunion he was expecting, but Sam didn't hesitate and ran after Paul. When he got to the room and saw Brett on the table, his heart sank. He washed his hands and put on some gloves. Then Sam went over and felt for a pulse on Brett, it was very weak. He asked, "How long is it been?"

"About forty-five minutes to an hour," Jason said.

Sam said, "Even if he were in the best hospital, he would need a miracle. I can try, but his odds are close to zero. I'm surprised he still alive."

Paul said, "What do you need?"

Sam said, "A lot of blood, scalpel, forceps, and a lot of luck. A miracle."

Paul shook his head and said, "I don't have any blood, I don't even know his blood type. Why didn't I think of that? I should have that information."

Sam felt for a pulse again and said, "It's too late. He's gone."

The room was silent for a few minutes until Jason spoke. He said, "It was my fault. I thought we were safe being so close to the entrance and left the safety of the trees to walk on the road."

Paul said, "I told you we didn't need to hear about that right now. You're still alive and you're still injured, so we need to worry about you."

Sam looked at Jason and for the first time saw that he did need help. He said, "You were hit too? Put Brett on the couch, Jason get on the table."

Jack and Paul moved Brett to the couch and Jason made his way to the table to replace him. Sam got to work on Jason.

Sam said, "How long were you going to sit there without telling me you needed medical care?"

Jason didn't answer. Sam told Paul what he would need and Paul gathered the equipment. They would not be able to put Jason to sleep, but a little morphine would help.

Jack felt useless and went out to greet the newcomers. He saw Sam's family and Josh. Josh was talking to Mark, who had filled them in on what happened.

Jack said, "Mark, would you be able to help Sam?"

Mark said, "Sure. I didn't think I was needed after the doctor arrived."

Jack said, "I think you'll be a better helper than Paul."

Mark nodded his head and left the room. Jack greeted the newcomers and tried to lighten the mood by asking about their ride here. A few minutes later Paul walked out and thanked Jack for keeping his company company. Paul took over and asked if they were hungry, then asked Tabatha to prepare some snacks.

Then Paul said, "Marie, I thought you only had two kids. Am I getting old or did you eat a magic bean?"

Marie said, "I'm sorry, this is Mercy. We met in Eatonville, she needed help, so we took her in. Maybe she'll tell you the story someday."

Paul nodded and turned to Josh. He knew enough not to push for Mercy's story at this time. He never had children, but he didn't have to be a parent to put two and two together.

Jack asked Josh if he brought any firepower.

Josh said, "It's me. I brought a few toys."

Paul said, "Good. We're going to need everything we've got."

Part III War

Muster

THE GENERAL SAT IN AN ABANDONED OFFICE NEAR THE river, waiting for his men to arrive. The ranger station was too small to hold everyone. There wasn't much use for these administration buildings at present, but they could use them for storage later. With the shooting of the two men, he wanted everybody on the same page. He greeted everyone as they walked in but did not stand up for anyone. He claimed it was his age that kept him from standing, but everyone knew it was his belly.

When everyone had arrived – minus Sgt. Jackson and the roving patrol – he began the meeting, still seated.

"Good morning everyone," he said. "I'm happy you could all get away from your busy careers to join us here today."

There were a few giggles, smirks, and shaking heads at the general's attempt at sarcasm.

He continued, "I'm sure you've all heard about the two men are patrol shot yesterday. We don't know what they were doing here or how long they were here. But the lieutenant found signs that someone was watching us from behind the ranger station. It could have been them or not. It could have been people from Cougar Rock or even Paradise. Although, I don't see too many people surviving at Paradise. It has good shelter but not enough food to hunt. The point here is someone is, or was, watching us. We need to be on guard, more aware of our surroundings. I also want an extra guard circling the area twenty-four hours a day. Whoever was watching, felt comfortable enough to sleep right behind my office. We can't let that happen again."

One of the men spoke up and said, "Me and John walked behind your office last night to take a pee and didn't see anyone. We walked a good distance away from the office, I don't think anyone was there. At least not last night."

The lieutenant said, "It was last night. Maybe you didn't walk far enough out, or you just weren't paying attention."

The man's face turned red, and he looked to the floor, but didn't say anything else.

The general spoke again, "If those two men have family or friends, they may come looking for their friends, or revenge. When we took over here, there was plenty of game. But now we need to go further out to find the food. We can't have people from outside the park coming in and taking our food. We shouldn't have to worry about Cougar Rock because of our deal with them. But there may come a day if they start running out of game. With our hunters out so far, it would be good if you could find out where those horses came from. We have stables here the horses would be a nice addition."

There were a few nervous looks around the room when the general suggested they steal horses.

Sgt. Baker said, "as far as we've been out, we have never seen a horse. It could be too Dangerous to go much further."

The general said, "We have bikes now, you can go farther. It can be anyone, it doesn't have to be the hunters. It *shouldn't* be the hunters. They should be hunting for food, not horses."

With that, the general dismissed the men. Sgt. Baker and Cpl. Isakson walked down the river to speak without being overheard. Neither of them liked the general anymore. He had become corrupt and dictatorial. They should have seen it coming back when he was elected to be the leader.

Sgt. Baker said, "Something needs to change here, and that something is the general. We need to get him out."

Cpl. Isakson said, "I agree, and it should've happened a long time ago. But it will take more than the two of us, who can we trust?"

"That is a great question. We need to recruit some others, and I have a few ideas about who would help. But if we asked the wrong person, it's over. If we're lucky, we'd only be tossed out. I have a better idea. We can volunteer to look for horses. The general said hunters shouldn't go, but I'll counter that I've been out into Ashford and know where not to look, saving time. But instead of looking for horses, we look for outside help. The people we've warned to stay away from the park would have a lot of incentive to help us."

Sgt. Baker was successful and got himself and Cpl. Isakson on the first team going out. The morning shift guards still had the bicycles, so they would leave at 4 PM. They each packed a backpack with a change of clothes, some food, their EDC, and a sleeping bag. It would be near dark by the time they reached Ashford, so they would make camp there and start the quest the next day. It would give them almost a full day to "look" for horses. They agreed not to talk to anyone about the plan before they left.

Baker and Isakson met at the ranger station at 3:50 PM to relieve the guards of their bicycles. The guards arrived just before 4 PM, and the two plotters made their way for Ashford. The ride was mostly flat but did have a slight downward slope, which made it an easy ride. They looked for a place in Ashford to make camp and chose the Mount Rainier visitor association. Even though it looked like a ghost town, this place was least likely to have anyone hanging around. It didn't escape them that they were also visitors. They walked behind the building and found a spot in the trees to make camp.

Sgt. Baker said, "I don't think we'll need to set a watch. I don't think anyone is around here anymore, but just in case, I'll stay up a little bit just to be sure."

Isakson said, "I'm not tired, so I'll stay up with you. What do you think about asking the redhead to join us? She can't fight, but she might be able to win people over. She's pretty, and everyone seems to like her. Especially the general, who likes her little too much. I'm sure she would like to see him gone."

Baker said, "I like the way you think. She would be a great asset, I'm sure. It wouldn't be difficult to talk her into it. You want to ask her, or should I?"

Isakson said, "I can. I don't think she views me as a threat because I'm much younger than she is. She talks to me like I'm her little brother."

Baker laughed and said, "Well I guess you're out of the lottery."

They talked for about an hour then decided to get some sleep. The next morning they built a small fire to heat up some water for the meal pouches. Then they got on their bikes to look for the home of the red haired lady he'd seen a few days ago. Sgt. Baker thought, *everyone's a redhead nowadays*. He knew the general area but was approaching it from the south instead of the east. They followed several roads and checked several driveways before finding the right one. An hour and 1/2 after breakfast they were standing in the right driveway. They mustered up the courage and made their way to the front door.

Barking dogs announce their arrival before they reached the door, however. They saw a face in the window, and both put their hands out to show they weren't holding weapons. Each of the men was armed, of course, but they wanted the people inside to know their hands were empty. A few seconds later the door opened, and the dogs rushed out. Baker and Isakson thought they were about to get attacked but before they could react the dog stopped and sat in front of each man. Then a man walked out carrying an AR-15. A redheaded woman walked out behind him, carrying a Glock.

The woman's eyes squinted a little and she said, "You're one of the men who said I could not hunt in the park,"

Sgt. Baker said, "You are correct. But that's not why we're here, or in a roundabout way, it is. We are here to ask for your help and make a deal."

Jack said, "Forgive my skepticism, but why the change of heart after only a few days? And why should we trust you just days after your people killed my friend?"

Baker said, "I had nothing to do with that and if you hear us out, you'll get your revenge."

Jack stood in silence for a few moments and said, "Keep talking."

Baker explained the power structure and how their leader became drunk with power and corrupt. He told of their desire for a coup and said if Jack and Diane helped, they would share the park for hunting. They would also get their revenge. It was the general who ordered us to shoot trespassers on sight. A few of us aren't following that order.

Jack and Diane listened intently, and Jack asked, "How many men with guns do you have?" He knew from Jason the number to be around fifteen, so the question was a test of their honesty.

Baker said, "We have 25 men, and one is down with an injury for now. I don't know when he'll be well enough to fight. A few men that aren't in our group but living there also have weapons. They will no doubt fight with us."

Jack said, "Our information said about 15 men."

Baker said, "Your information probably did not account for our hunters."

Baker offered some more information and said, "We are a bunch of survivalists. We just happened to be in the park practicing winter survival when all this went down. Every one of us is proficient with our weapons, and I think most will be against us. This won't be an easy fight, unless you can find a few other people to help. But the general needs to go. Isakson and I still have the morals he seems to have lost, and I think a few more of us do too. We have a plan to find out who's with us without exposing ourselves. So, we should have a little more help. Are you in?"

Jack said, "I'll talk to a few people and see if I can recruit them. Check back here in two weeks, that should give us both enough time to see how much help we would have."

Baker said, "Sounds good. We'll see you in two weeks."

Baker and Isakson turned around and left while Jack and Diane watched. When the two men were out of earshot Jack said, "So what do you think?"

Diane said, "It sounds too good to be true."

"That's what I thought too."

Preparation

JACK RELAYED ALL THE NEW INFORMATION TO PAUL. PAUL was excited and didn't share too much of Jack and Diane's skepticism. He may have been too bent on revenge to consider a trap. Paul wanted everyone together for a special meeting at Paul's house. Paul and Jason were still recovering and would not make it to the normal meeting hall. It meant some of the members would have to travel a lot farther than normal, but the meeting had to happen. He gave everyone two days' notice so they can make preparations. Ranger John would be at this meeting in person, so Paul sent two men on horses to escort him. John had his own horse, but Paul didn't want anyone traveling alone.

Jack and Diane arrived 15 minutes early, and Paul was outside to greet them.

Jack said, "I see you're here first again."

Both men laughed and Diane looked a little confused.

Paul said, "Go on inside. Jason, Josh, and Sam are all inside waiting."

Jack said, "Why don't you come in too? Nobody expects you to stand outside in the cold."

Paul winked and said, "But *I expect me* to greet everyone."

Jack shook his head and laughed, then went inside. He greeted everyone and asked Sam where his family was.

Sam said, "Martha and Larry took them on a tour of the property that will end in the picnic. That got them out of here so we can discuss whatever we need to."

Jack said, "Great idea. I'm sure the kids will love the animals. Tell them not to get too close to the pigs, I could use some of that bacon."

Sam laughed and said, "Will do, we all like bacon too."

Nikki walked in and greeted everyone. She said to Mark, "I have someone for you to train with the sniper rifle. She's very good with what I've been able to teach her, but I'm not a sniper. Paul agrees she has the talent and we think you can turn her into a great sniper."

Mark said, "Sounds great. I still need to get settled in, but I can start whenever she's ready. Who is she?"

"Her name is Robin and she will be here later, after the meeting. She's not one of us yet, but I think she will be soon."

"I can't wait to meet her," Mark said.

The small gathering talked amongst themselves until everyone had arrived, and Paul came inside to start the meeting.

Paul said, "First, I'd like to thank everyone who attended Brett's funeral. I've had a spot reserved for a small graveyard for a long time, and was hoping not to use it for a much longer time. His death is the reason for this meeting. We will get revenge, but not today. One, they'd be expecting something soon. We aren't gonna run in there, guns blazing, and fall into that trap. No, we're going to plan this out. We will be prepared, and we will clean that rats nest out."

A few people nodded their heads, a few clapped, and a few cheered.

Paul continued, "We have the intelligence Jason and Brett collected. We have a source from inside Longmire that approached Jack and Diane. It turns out the leadership at Longmire isn't loved by everyone, and a few people are ready for a coup. We will help make that happen. We don't know how many people will be helping from the inside. So far, the number is two. We do know they have twenty-five armed men, only the men armed. So only men are our targets. That information came from the inside. Jason counted 12 to 15 men and confirmed no women were caring weapons."

"The source said the hunters could explain the discrepancy in the numbers. They were out hunting," Jack said.

Jason said, "They have a twenty-four-hour watch. They ride bicycles on patrol and change guards every eight hours, 8 AM, 4 PM, and midnight. They wore night vision goggles after dark. I only saw the active patrol wearing them, so I don't know how many goggles they have."

Paul said, "I'm going to get in touch with Morton and ask them for help. I'd like them to cover the river to prevent any of the targets escaping or trying to circle around and attack us from behind. John is going to bring a few people from Elbe to help out. I will also call Eatonville to ask for help. I want to go in with overwhelming force."

John said, "Thanks for the escort here. I would probably still be looking for your house without them. I'm sure I can get a few volunteers considering most of them would be dead if it weren't for your help."

"No worries. I didn't want you traveling alone, I don't want *anyone* traveling alone anymore. It's getting too Dangerous. Do you have another horse?"

"I only have this one. When we evacuated the park, we took the horses with us. But other rangers have the other horses."

"No problem. I will send you home with an extra horse and the escort. For future meetings, bring a friend."

Paul said, "Mark, are we set with night vision goggles?"

Mark said, "I've got a few, and I can get more, but that means a trip to my shop and house. With a few vehicles, I can bring enough weapons, body armor, night vision goggles, ammo, and everything else we need. With three or four trucks we'll be well stocked for a long time."

Jack said, "I have a truck but not enough gas."

"Don't worry about gas, I've got enough," Paul said. "This is a good idea, I like it. We'll set a day for another meeting to discuss those plans. We've got a little bit of time as we wait for the source inside to recruit a few more people. Okay, next up is our new arrivals. I'm ecstatic to have Josh and Sam with us. I know everyone was worried about them and someday you'll have to hear the story from them. It's quite a tale. Sam and his family are going to stay here for the time being. He's got a well-equipped office here, so if anyone needs medical attention, you know where we live."

He continued, "Josh will be moving into his cabin, which means Jack's friends will have to go back to Jack's place. We'll need a few volunteers to help with the move again. There shouldn't be any fireworks this time, however."

Jack said, "Great, I miss them. They'll be a big help with security too. Being on the park border is usually a good thing, but at present, I'll take the extra guns."

Paul nodded and said, "Last on the list, everyone should beef up their home defenses. Things are only going to get worse. Everyone have a safe trip home."

Diane said, "I need to speak to the doctor while we're here."

Jack said, "Are you okay?

"I'm fine, just a little sick. I want to see what I've got."

"Okay, I'll be out here. Take your time."

Diane asked the doctor for a moment, and they went to his office. Nikki approached Josh and asked him to come outside, Robin should be waiting. Outside, they spotted Robin on a porch swing and approached.

Nikki said, "Hello Robin, it's good to see you again. I've missed you."

Robin stood and said, "Hello my friend, I've missed you too!"

The two women embraced then Nikki said, "This is Josh, our sniper, gunsmith, and gun dealer all rolled into one. He's going to finish your training, I've done all I can do. Josh, this is Robin."

Josh said, "Hello Robin, I've heard good things about you and your talent. Two people I have a ton of respect for say you're a prodigy."

Robin said, "Prodigy? I don't know about that."

Josh laughed, "I may have embellished, but they said you have talent. We can't do any hands-on training until I get settled into my cabin, but we can sit on the swing and discuss things. A porch swing in the middle of all this seems so out of place, but peaceful."

Nikki said, "I'll leave you two alone," and walked back inside.

Diane sat on the table in the doctor's office and told him about her morning sickness and being hungry all the time.

"I've been told by a few doctors I can't get pregnant, so that's not why I'm getting sick. But it is crazy it happens every morning."

Sam said, "This may come as a shock, but sometimes doctors are wrong. We're human and sometimes rely too much on what we know. We forget about things we don't know, like why women who shouldn't get pregnant - get pregnant. I've seen enough cases of pregnant women who can't get pregnant to know you *just* might be pregnant."

Diane's heart sank. She didn't want to finally get pregnant in the middle of whatever these times were. She's always wanted children, but this environment isn't suitable for babies. She should be elated, but only felt dread.

Sam said, "Here's an EPT, run off to the bathroom and let's see what it says. Diane returned a few minutes later. She held it up to Sam to show a positive result. Sam smiled but saw the tears in her eyes. She explained she was happy but sad at the same time, and told him her reservations. He did his best to reassure her, and she feigned a happy face for him.

Sam said, "The sooner you tell Jack, the better you'll feel. I'm sure he'll be happy, and he can help you through this."

"I will. Soon. I have to figure it out myself first."

"I understand. You aren't showing yet, so you have some time. Come see me in four weeks for a checkup, okay?"

"Okay, I'll be here. Thanks."

She took a few minutes to compose herself. She saw the basin and pitcher of water and washed her face. Diane didn't want Jack to know she had cried. She wouldn't be able to explain that away. Then she joined Jack in the living room. She walked up to him with a smile.

Jack said, "How did it go?"

Diane said, "Okay, I'm going to be better soon."

"Okay, good to hear. Are you ready to go?"

"Yes, let's get home."

Moving Out

ON MOVING DAY, JACK AND DIANE MET EVERYONE AT Paul's house. Paul would be staying home this time, however. Jason would miss this move as well. He still needed more time to heal. The others joining the moving party were Mark, Robin and her husband Mark, and a few others. Larry would drive the wagon. Thirty minutes after Jack and Diane arrived, they were on their way. Diane and Robin rode in the wagon. Josh drove behind the wagon so the horses and everyone else didn't breathe his exhaust. Diane still had not told Jack about being pregnant, but made an excuse to ride instead of walk. Her and Robin made small talk along the way.

Diane said, "You've come a long way from when I first met you, crying on the side of the road, alone in your car."

Robin said, "That feels like so long ago. It's hard to believe it's just been three or four months, I lose track of time now though."

Diane said, "Losing track of time is easy to do now, I

completely understand. We have a calendar at the cottage but its days are numbered."

Robin laughed and said, "Pun intended?"

"Absolutely."

They arrived at Josh's cabin and Josh said, "Home sweet home." Ralph and Brandon had been expecting them and opened the door when they heard the horse and wagon. They had everything packed and ready to go, so it was only a matter of loading the wagon. Josh said, "Thanks for keeping her safe for me."

Ralph said, "Don't mention it. It's a nice place. It could use a TV, but it's a nice place."

Brandon said, "I just finished chopping up a cord of wood for the fireplace, so you'll be good there for a while."

Josh said, "You must be Brandon. Jack speaks highly of you. Keep up the hard work and maybe you'll be leading us one day."

Brandon smiled and looked to the ground and shook his head a few times. Jack said, "Let's get this show on the road. Load up and get back to Paul's so everyone can get home before dark." It didn't take long to get everything loaded up. The numbers were for safety, not carrying loads. They helped Josh unload his Bronco. He didn't have much but what he had was heavy. When they finished, Josh thanked everyone and told them to hang tight for just a second. He fished around a few footlockers before finding what he was looking for.

Josh said, "You worked hard here Brandon and I can't let you walk away empty-handed. Take this as compensation."

He handed Brandon a Walther PPS M2 Laser.

Brandon's eyes grew wide in his mouth hung open. After a few seconds he said, "Thanks! This might be too much. This is a 9mm, right?"

Josh smiled and said, "You bet. Here's a holster for it too. Do you need some ammo?"

Before Brandon could answer, Josh was digging around again and came back with a box of 9mm hollow point rounds and handed them to Brandon.

Brandon said, "Geez man, thanks. I don't know what to say."

Josh said "There's nothing to say. You earned it."

They said their goodbyes and made their way to Jack's cottage. Once there they unloaded and got everything inside. There were more farewells as the helper crew made their way home. The crew hitched a ride as far as Larry could take them before walking the rest of the way to their homes. Mark rode to Paul's with Larry so he wouldn't be alone. Horses were huge a target for thieves.

Back home, Diane prepared a meal and Jack helped his friends get unpacked.

Jack said, "It's good to have you guys back. It makes the days go by quicker when I have more people to talk to. I love Diane, but sometimes we just run out of things to say."

Ralph said, "It was getting that way at Josh's cabin too. I'll be glad for the extra conversation as well. This kid is too smart for me and uses too many big words."

They all laughed.

Brandon said, "I tried to use the time to teach dad how to cook, but it was useless. It's best to keep him away from the kitchen until we can use a microwave again."

Jack filled them in on the Longmire situation and said they needed to be on their guard while they're outside.

Jack said, "They shoot first. But we're going to shoot last."

Ralph said, "When is this going to go down?"

Jack said, "We've got a few weeks. We're waiting on some intelligence and we're going to make a run to Puyallup for supplies. Josh has a heavy stash of weapons that we need to recover."

Brandon said, "He's got more than what he has in the footlockers? I thought that was a lot already."

Jack laughed and said, "You would not believe how much he has. He owns a gun store, he's a gun collector, and we've been giving him money to stockpile weapons for us. When he didn't show up after the attack, we assumed he was dead and we'd never see those weapons. It was a huge blow. He is also a nice guy, so we would miss that too. But we really needed those weapons."

Diane told them to quit jabbering and come eat.

Julie

Julie was in her room combing her hair when there was a knock at the door. She put her brush down and answered. Cpl. Isakson was there and asked if he could come in. Julie stepped aside and waved him in.

"Hi, I'm Cpl. Isakson. But you can call me Craig, I'm tired of all these military titles. I'm not here for any healing, but I do hope you can help me."

Julie cocked her eyebrows and said, "What do you have in mind?"

Craig glanced at her son and whispered, "I know you don't like the general and you have good reason. I don't like him either, and I know at least one other. I've recruited some outside help to take him down. I know there are more of us that wouldn't mind seeing him gone, but it's too dangerous for me to ask. You're a pretty woman, and a lot of the guys here are smitten. You could make them talk by giving them a little attention. They will want to impress you."

Julie said, "If it's too dangerous for you, it would be too

dangerous for me also. And don't worry about my son, he won't talk."

Craig said, "No, you aren't going to ask them to join me. That would be dangerous for both of us. I only need you to see how people feel about him. I have an idea of who would help and those are the people I'd like you to talk to. I know who won't help, so don't ask anyone who isn't on this list."

He handed Julie a list of names and she read them over.

She said, "I talk to this one every day and he has loose lips. He's one that thinks he has a chance with me, but I'll tell you, anyone who has hit on me knowing my husband recently died has zero chance. Ever. A woman needs to grieve. I'll see him later today and ask a few questions. The rest may take me a few days to get to."

Craig said, "I can't thank you enough. Sgt. Baker or I will come back in three days to see what you've learned. If you talk to them all before then, you can find me in room five."

Julie said, "Okay, three days or sooner."

Julie walked him to the door and saw him out. She looked over the list again to memorize the names. Then she crumpled it up and threw it in the pee bucket. Julie finished brushing her hair and got dressed to check in on her patient. Yesterday they were able to move him out of the Ranger station and to his room. She told her son not to open the door for anyone and went to see Sgt. Jackson. *He does have loose lips*, she thought. He told her that most of them were never in the military, but use the ranks to show positions and how long a person has been with them. So Rufino was right about something and isn't completely useless. She arrived at his door and knocked. She heard someone say, "Come in, it's not locked."

She opened the door and walked in and Sgt. Jackson didn't waste any time. He said, "Hello beautiful. I finally got you in my room." On the inside she sighed, but right now she needed him, so she smiled and said, "Now now, this is a professional visit, and you're too injured even to answer the door. So, how are you feeling?"

"The same as yesterday, I guess. My back is cramping up a little today though."

Julie saw her chance and took it. She told him his back is cramping because the muscles were compensating for his gut being torn open and repairing itself. She did not know if that was true, but he didn't either. She wanted to get him talking, and a relaxing massage would do the trick.

She said, "Roll over on your belly and I'll give you a massage. Don't get cute, it's a professional visit."

Jackson said, "Oh, bummer. Maybe next time."

Maybe never, she thought.

He rolled over and she started to massage his muscled back. Her pale hands contrasted against his ebony skin. For the first few minutes she didn't say anything. She wanted him to get comfortable and relaxed before pulling information out of him. Then she said, "How do you feel about the general?"

He said, "Why? Are you going to dump me and take him up on his offer?"

Julie said, "There will never be a day where I let that man put his hands on me. I'm really in awe that so many grown men listen to him."

Jackson said, "Did you know he was a high school janitor before this started? That's pretty far from being a general. He got the position mostly because he had the most seniority in our survivalist group. He was a pretty likable guy too, once upon a time. The guy you see today isn't the same guy he was a few months ago."

Julie said, "So you don't like him anymore?"

He said, "There isn't much to like. The power has gone to his head and he thinks he's God now. He's done some awful things and some of those things I don't participate in."

Julie said, "Like what?"

Jackson said, "Like the brothel. Those women aren't there because they want to be, they're there because he gave them a choice that wasn't a choice. I'm not the only one who won't go in there. Some of us still have our values. You're lucky you can heal. You're the prettiest girl here and you can bet he wants you in the brothel, or worse. I bet he's trying to get you for himself."

Julie felt herself getting hot and knew her face must've been three shades of red. She was doing her best to keep her composure, but it was hard knowing this man and the others weren't doing anything to help those women. She took a long, deep breath before speaking again.

Julie said, "It sounds to me like he's gone over the edge. Do you all just rubber stamp his decisions? Maybe if he got some blow-back on his stupid decisions, he wouldn't be this bad. Have you thought about voting for someone else?"

Jackson said, "At this point, everyone is too afraid to say anything. They have the numbers."

That was all Julie could take and she needed to leave before she exploded. She said, "I'll be back tomorrow, no jumping jacks." She got to the door and turned around then said, "I'm nobody's whore. The sooner that pig realizes it, the better off we'll all be." She walked out the door.

She grabbed her coat from her room then left the inn to get some fresh air and calm herself down. She hoped to see one or more of the men on her list as she walked but instead, things went from bad to worse. She spotted the general and changed directions. She did not feel like getting ogled by a second man today. She was too late, however, the general had seen her and called her over. *Just my luck*, she thought. He only leaves the Ranger station to eat, and she had to walk out during mealtime. She turned around and walked over to him with a fake smile on her face.

The general smiled and said, "Hello Julie, you're looking pretty today. How was Sgt. Jackson?"

Julie said, "How can you tell under my hood?" It was a small job to let him know what he said was stupid. Then she said, "He's recovering well and should be on his feet soon."

He said, "That's good to hear, he's a good man."

Then the general grabbed Julie's hands and stroked the top of her wrists with his thumbs. She tried to pull her hands away, but he held firm.

The general said, "I think you know what I want. I can make your life here much easier and make sure you and your son get more food. All you have to do is share my bed."

Julie said, "As you know, I'm still grieving for my late husband. Furthermore, nobody can buy me. A man must earn me, not pay me."

With that, she got her hands free and walked away. The general watched as she moved through the parking lot then turned and returned to his office. The colonel was there alone and the general asked, "What do you think of Julie? She's pretty, but do we really need her? We all know a little, or a lot, about natural medicine. We've all got some supplies. Maybe we can cut her loose."

The colonel thought for a moment and said, "I think we should wait and see. She's doing good with Sgt. Jackson and we should at least let him heal first. Plus, we must think about the men we shot. If anyone comes seeking revenge, will need all the healing we can get. Let's wait it out and see what happens. If nobody comes for us, we can dispose of her and her son.

⚜

Julie walked as fast as she could to get away from the general. She got to a cabin and walked behind it then stopped to compose herself. Tears had welled up in her eyes, a mixture of anger and sadness. Someone was in the cabin and saw her through the window. He walked out of the cabin looked around the corner and asked if she was okay.

She said, "I will be, I just need a few minutes." Then she recognized him as one of the men on the list. She said, "Is it okay if I regain my composure inside?"

"Of course you can, come on in."

They went inside and made small talk for a few minutes. Then Julie started to warm the man up.

She said, "I'm sorry I'm such a mess, the general won't leave me alone. He knows I just lost my husband but is still trying to get me in his bed. He thinks I'm a prostitute and can be bought for food. He won't take no for an answer." She gave him her best sad, pouty look.

Lieutenant Thurber said, "You are in a bad position, and you need to be careful with him. It might be best for you to avoid him at all costs."

Julie said, "I tried to avoid him today, but I wasn't fast enough. What do you think of him?"

He said, "That's tough. We're all still alive, so there's that. But some of the things he's done tick me off. I think one day he will go too far and get replaced. But for now, we have to live with his decisions. But if he puts his hands on you again, come talk to me. That is not okay."

Julie heard what she needed to hear and thanked him for making her feel better. She left and went back to her room.

Making Plans

JACK, JOSH, JASON, AND MARK SAT IN PAUL'S LIVING ROOM to discuss the mission to Puyallup. They were worried about Jason, but he said he would be fine. They needed his truck and driving isn't taxing. He said, "You guys can do the heavy lifting, I'll supervise. Besides, I keep telling you the wound isn't bad."

Paul said, "You're going to pick up John in Elbe and another truck and Eatonville. They'll provide the driver and a few more men. The driver will have his own night vision goggles. While you're there, you can top off the gas tanks. One of the members owns a gas station. Their help will be free, however. We'll have to give them some supplies, but that won't be an issue. We need the truck and the manpower. Okay Josh, the floor is yours."

Josh said, "I don't think I've ever had the floor, I like it. Okay, the short story is I have some supplies at the shop and a mini arsenal stored at my house. Some of it I bought myself, but most of it was paid for by Paul and donations from the members. It's a given that my shop has been broken into by now. But that's okay, if or when they get into the safe the find a little cash, a grenade, and two handguns. They'll think they scored, but the grenade is a dummy, and the handguns don't work. But it should satisfy them enough to not look for the real stash. They would need a metal detector to find, however. The stash is buried behind my shop. The bigger stash is an old fallout shelter behind my house. That was the selling point for me. I knew exactly what to do with the fallout shelter."

Jack said, "So what do you, or we, have stashed there."

Josh replied, "Ha ha, you're going to be surprised. All told, there are more night vision goggles, some body armor, for AR-15's, converted to full automatic, 3 M249's - also known as SAW's - and I have another one at the cabin, two Barret Model 98B's, grenades and flashbangs. I have three more footlockers full of AR-15's, handguns, ammo, some C4, a few Claymore's, bows and all the paraphernalia, and the reloader. I have a bow press at home... at the cabin I mean, that will take some getting used to. And I think Paul has a press here too."

Paul said, "Yes, the bow presses set up in the warehouse. With the reloader coming, will need to have everyone start saving their brass."

Mark said, "That is a lot of firepower. How much body armor is there? Where did you get the explosives?"

Josh said, "There is enough for everyone and then some. Got some spare plates too. But don't get too cocky wearing it, your head is still squishy. It's still better to have it than not, just don't use it as a crutch. It doesn't make you invincible. About my sources... I'm a man of many talents."

Jack said, "Okay, so we meet here and pick up John. Drive to

Eatonville for gas and an extra truck. Then what, the store or your house?"

Josh said, "The store is closer so we should go there first. My house isn't too far from the store, however."

Jack said, "Good. Then we jet back to Eatonville to top off the tanks, take John home, then back to Paul's. I assume our Eatonville friends will sleep at Paul's before returning home, correct?"

Paul said, "Yes. They will sleep here, and we'll choose some goodies for them in the morning before they leave."

Jack said, "I can see why you built such a big house now. You have a lot of guests."

Paul said, "You'll be traveling at night without lights, and each driver will be wearing night vision goggles. Stay on the road, and you'll be fine. So, did we miss anything?"

Josh said, "My shop is on Meridian, and while I doubt it sees the traffic it used to, it's still the main road through Puyallup and might see some sort of traffic. We need to set a few guards so we don't get surprised. We are bound to draw some attention if people are up after dark anymore."

Paul said, "Sounds like a plan. If there's nothing else, we can break up and I'll see everyone here again in two days. Be here by 4 PM for last-minute instructions and to gas up. You can leave here before dark but don't go past Elbe until after dark. Jack, stick around for minute if you can, I need to talk to you."

Jack said, "Sure thing, boss."

They waited a few minutes for everyone to go home then Paul took Jack to the communication room. It was a good place for a private conversation. Paul sat on the chair, and Jack found a comfortable spot on the windowsill. Jack said, "I trust you didn't forget to show me something here, so what's on your mind?"

Paul said, "You're right, nothing new here. I wanted to talk to you about your informant, Baker wasn't it? In my initial excitement, I forgot to ask if you trust him. It's been gnawing at me for the past few days."

Jack said, "I trust him as much as I can. I tested him with questions I already knew the answers to, or thought knew the answers to. He impressed me with the number of men they had. If he would have said less than twelve, then I would've considered him untrustworthy. But he almost doubled what we thought they had. So, he told the truth there at least. I think we can plan an attack with his information and the help he says he'll provide. But, we need to have a backup plan just in case. We'll have the numbers and I'm pretty sure they can't match our firepower, especially with the new supplies we're about to pick up."

Paul said, "Good, that makes me feel better. Brett was a good guy and I let my bloodlust take over and prevent my brain from thinking. I still want revenge, but now that I've had time to think about it, I'm able to see the mistakes I was making. That's why it's never good to react immediately. Think with your brain, not your heart. I should have a sign made. Maybe there's a place in Ashford?"

Both men laughed at the little joke, needing it with the seriousness of the conversation. Then Paul said, "Well, I guess you should get home to the pretty little lady. Are you taking her to Puyallup?"

Jack got up and as he was walking out of the room said, "No.

She hasn't been feeling well lately so I'll ask Ralph to come with me. I'd like Brandon to go too, but I'd feel better with two people at the cottage."

Paul said, "Good idea. It's safer that way."

They went downstairs, and Jack said his goodbyes then made his way home.

Survivor Alliance

SGT. BAKER LEFT THE INN AND WAS HEADED FOR THE
Ranger station when he saw someone he needed to talk to.
He picked up his pace to intercept him without screaming his
name and drawing attention to them. He had a bucket and it
looked like his target was headed for the river, so he chose his
angle and quick-stepped his way over. When he was close
enough, he said, "Hey James, how's it going?"

"Hi Scott, what's up?"

Baker said, "Are you joining us on the next hunt? I noticed
you weren't at the last one."

James said, "Yeah I'll be there. I had a migraine before the
last one and stayed in bed. How did you do?"

He said, "We bagged a deer and a few rabbits. So it was okay.
So, what do you think of the general's new policy? Shoot first
and ask questions later."

James said, "I've never shot anybody, and I hope I never have to. It makes me wonder if he ever got out of the office if he would think the same."

Baker said, "I hear ya there. I was hoping the colonel could talk him down from that one, but he either didn't try or didn't succeed. There are a few rules I would change if I had the power to do so."

James said, "I agree. Sometimes I just don't understand what's going on in his head."

Baker said, "I wish we could do something about it, but what I don't know."

James remembered he was at the river to collect some water and walked across a log to get clean water without getting wet. Being careful not to slip or fall in, he bent down and dipped his bucket in to fill it up. Then he walked back to shore to finish the conversation. He said, "I don't know either. I wish I had the answer, but right now I've got to purify some of this and shave with the rest of it."

Baker said, "I understand. I'll see you soon."

❧

Sgt. Baker and Cpl. Isakson took a walk across the river, crossing the bridge at Longmire. Nobody was going to over-hear them that far away. After crossing, they walked a few minutes downriver to be sure. Then Sgt. Baker said, "I talked to Scott this morning and got a good vibe off him. I think we'll be able to trust him, so we can add him to the list. How did you do?"

Isakson said, "I talked to Perry and Schon, and I think they're good. But, Pineda is out. He had too many good things to say about the general. I think he may even be worse than the general."

Baker said, "That's a scary thought. I will speak to Julie later and see if she's made progress. I'll add these three names to her list, and she can dig deeper. I've talked to a few more that are no-gos. Everyone else I wouldn't consider approaching. I could be wrong, but it's too risky. We should head back."

They turned and headed back to Longmire. Isakson had a guard shift coming up and needed to get ready. Baker headed to Julie's room to speak with her. He would speak in whispers again to keep from being overheard. People would get the wrong idea if they saw the two of them walking off alone. More than a few of the men would get jealous seeing that, one being the general. He got to her door and knocked. She opened the door and said, "Hello, Scott. Come in." He stepped in, and they made small talk for a few minutes before getting down to business.

Baker whispered, "How did you do?"

Julie whispered back, "Jackson and Thurber are good. So are Peters and O'Malley. I would not trust Thomas. He gives me the creeps."

Baker said, "That's good to hear, thanks. I have a few more names for you, and we warmed them up. Don't speak to anyone else hear about it. They've all been ruled out. Talking to anyone else could be dangerous."

"I understand. Is there anything else?"

"That's it for now, I guess. I'll check back soon."

Sgt. Baker left Julie's room and grabbed a fishing pole and some gear from his room. He didn't have anything else to do until tomorrow and went to try for some fresh trout from the river.

☙❧

The next day, Baker and Isakson volunteered to search for horses again and took the bikes from the 4 PM shift. It was earlier than planned, but they felt they had enough information and the sooner the general was gone, the better. They stopped at the visitor center again and made camp behind it. Once again, they stayed awake and talked for about an hour after dark and went to sleep without setting a watch. The next morning, they had a quick breakfast and made their way to Jack's cottage.

It did not take too long this time because they knew how to get there by road now. The dogs announced their arrival again, then Jack opened the door and said, "You're early. Is that good or bad?"

Baker said, "It's good. I think we have all the information we'll need."

This time Jack invited them inside to talk. Standing out in the cold wasn't too much fun. They got inside and sat down, then Jack got right to it. "So, what's the good news?"

Baker said, "So far we have four more people that want the general gone. We're looking into three more, and I'm pretty confident that they will be with us. So, the twenty-five men are down to sixteen and nine of us will be ready to fight. How many did you come up with?"

Jack said, "I'll be there, my friend Ralph will be there, and I've talked to a few neighbors. We will have more than them, the neighborhood is riled up."

Baker said, "I can't blame them. I'd be upset if someone told me I couldn't hunt to survive, and killed my neighbors."

Jack said, "What kind of weapons will we be facing?"

Baker said, "Everyone has an AR-15, at least one. Some of us have various hunting rifles, the standard varieties... 30-06, 308, you know, standard stuff. We've got handguns too, mostly 45s and 9mm's. Nothing fancy, just what we need to survive. We are survivalists, after all."

Jack said, "Fair enough. I think we can overcome that. You all know what each other look like, we do not. How are we to know who's on our side and who is not?"

Baker said, "That's a good question. I hadn't thought of that. We will have to come up with something."

Isakson said, "What about our hats? Nobody wears them anymore. That bright red stands out at a time we all want camouflage to blend in."

Baker said, "Good idea, that might work. We all have these red hats with our group name on them. They say, Survivor Alliance."

Jack smirked and Diane giggled.

Baker said, "I know. Original, right? I didn't pick the name, I just roll with it. But the hats should work. We will stand out and my friend here is right, nobody wears them anymore."

Jack said, "Okay, but tell them to be very careful where they are pointing their weapons. That plan isn't foolproof, so I'm a little wary. If someone in a red hat points a weapon at us, we will have no choice but to shoot."

Baker said, "I understand, and I will make sure everyone

knows. I can't think of another way to tell us apart, so this will have to do. So, when do we do this?"

Jack wouldn't tell them the real date for two reasons: one, he didn't know and two, he still doesn't trust them enough. He said, "I don't know when we'll attack yet, but you'll know when it starts. We will come in guns blazing. It will start with sniper fire and escalate from there. So, you'll know it's us."

Baker said, "Do you have a rough estimate? Will need to have the hats on before you arrive. Otherwise, you may shoot one or more of us. I don't want to start wearing them until the time is near because it will draw suspicion."

Jack said, "Hmm... You have a point, and I wish I could give you a straight answer, but I just don't know. I will say between six and ten days from now. At that time, do not go outside without a red hat that says, Survivor Alliance."

Baker said, "Fair enough. That will give us six days to come up with a reason for wearing the hats, should anyone ask. Never volunteer information."

Jack stood and said, "Okay, we will see you in 6 to 10 days."

The two guests stood, and Baker said, "Oh I should tell you, if any of your friends have horses, they should hide and protect them. We are supposed to be out looking for horses to steal, and we aren't the only ones who have been sent out on this mission."

Jack thanked him for the information and the two men left. Jack sat right down and sent a message to Paul:

I just talked to the two men from Longmire. They have a total of nine on our side. They will be wearing red hats. They are supposed to be looking for horses to steal and others are looking too. Guard your horses well until we take them out. I told them we will attack in 6 to 10 days.

Paul sent a message right back:

Good. Let's make it seven days. I'll relay the info to Morton. We won't see them until after the attack. Thanks for the info on the horses.

Baker and Isakson returned to Longmire after dark and set the bicycles against the Ranger station. As they were walking to the inn to get to their rooms, James approached and said, "Hey Scott, do you have a minute?"

Baker said, "I'm pretty tired and need to get some sleep, but sure, we can talk for a minute."

Isakson said, "I'll see you both tomorrow," and headed to his room.

James and Baker walked away from the inn making small talk till they were out of earshot. Then the conversation turned.

James said, "Did you send that redhead after me?"

Baker said, "What do you mean?" He was trying to stall for time so he could think.

James said, "Our conversation a few days ago is what I mean. Earlier today she struck up a conversation along the same lines. That can't be a coincidence."

Baker lied and said, "I haven't talked to her so whatever she said was her own doing."

James said, "Liar. I knew it was you. She said she talked to you. You want to take over, don't you?"

"I'm not trying to take over. Just like I told you, I'm hoping we can talk some sense into the general."

James pulled his sidearm and pointed it at Baker's chest. "I don't believe you."

Baker said, "You are making a mistake. You..."

As he was talking, James' eyes grew wide and his mouth hung open. He tried to speak but no words came out. Then he fell. Isakson was behind him and running up to Baker. Then he pulled the knife from James' back.

Baker said, "Nice throw and great timing. How did you know?"

Isakson said, "Julie caught me in the hallway and told me James knew and he was mad. She said he was going to tell the general you were planning to take over."

Baker said, "Well, I guess I called that one wrong. I thought he was with us. We need to do something with his body, however."

Isakson said, "Of course, but first am taking his gun and holster. I think I earned it."

They dragged the man across the street and onto the Trail of Shadows. Isakson ran back to his room and grabbed some duct tape and ran back. Then they found a large boulder and use the whole role to tape it to his belly. It wouldn't hold forever but with luck it would hold long enough. Then they rolled him into one of the hot Springs. When that was done, they finally made it to their rooms and got a good night sleep.

Puyallup

JACK AND RALPH PULLED INTO PAUL'S DRIVEWAY AND parked up close to the house. He would be filling his tank and wanted to be as close as possible. Jason's truck was ready to go, but Mark and Josh hadn't arrived yet. Jack wished everyone else shared his belief about showing up early. Paul was outside waiting, of course. "Good evening," Paul said. "Let's get that truck filled up."

Jack said, "Hello, Paul. Hello, Jason. It's a fine night for a drive. How are you feeling? Are you still up to drive?"

Jason said, "It's just a little pain, nothing I can't handle. There's no infection and Sam cleared me to go."

"That's good to hear," Jack said.

They got Jack's truck filled up, and a few minutes later Josh pulled in the driveway with Mark riding shotgun. Jack said, "Carpool, post-apocalypse style. We're all here. Get yourself gassed up and we can roll."

Paul said, "Keep your CB's on channel ten so we can hear if

you run into any problems. If you get split up meet at Josh's house. You've all got directions and the address. If you get split up on the way back, head for Ashford and try to coordinate a meeting place so you can stay grouped up."

Jack said, "Okay, I've got Ralph and Mark is riding with Jason. Josh, John will ride with you. Are we ready to roll?"

Josh said, "Give me two minutes and I should be done filling up."

Josh finished gassing up and handed night vision goggles to Jack and Jason. He had two more, one for himself and one as a backup. He'd already tested all the units, but anything can happen. They all got in their vehicles and made their way to Elbe. Jack put a CD in the player and the words of CW McCall blared out of the speakers. Ralph said, "Convoy. Appropriate." Jack just smiled. It didn't take long to reach Elbe in their vehicles. John waved to Jack and approached the truck. Jack rolled down the window and told him he's riding with Josh, "Jump in the Bronco, we're pairing up."

It wasn't quite dark yet, so they waited fifteen minutes before moving on to Eatonville. Jack gave a light tap on the horn and they were on their way. According to the plan, they drove with no lights. It was slow at first as Jack and Jason had never used night vision before. As time went on, they got more confident and were able to pick up the pace. They still weren't breaking any speed records, however. Their top speed was 40 miles an hour. After Eatonville, the road straightens out and they'll be able to move faster. Even so, it didn't take too long to reach Eatonville.

They had agreed to meet at Richards gas station. Josh knew where it was, having filled up there before. As they pulled in, Jack was relieved to see people waiting there for them. He was also glad to see the truck they would be driving. It was a big box truck. They were not going to have to leave anything behind. Richard had the pumps ready, and it didn't take long to top off the tanks. Jack saw his friend Calvin and asked if he was coming along.

Calvin said, "No, this mission is a young man's game. Up all night and carrying heavy objects? Not for this old man, thanks"

Jack said, "Those chickens are a real lifesaver, even with the two extra mouths to feed."

Calvin smiled and said, "I'm glad they're working out for you."

They only stayed long enough to fill up and make sure the Eatonville crew knew the plan, and what channel to be on. Once that was taken care of, they were on the road again. Their driver said he was experienced with night vision so they would not have to slow down for him. Jack was relieved. They passed the sign for Northwest Trek and Ralph said, "I bet there's some good hunting in there." Jack laughed and said, I bet there was a time, I also bet that time is gone and it's been hunted out." Northwest Trek is, or was, a large wildlife Park with herds of deer and elk. There were also a few moose, some bear, and various other animals.

Now they reached the straighter roads and were able to pick up the pace. Jack was in front and took them up to 50 miles an hour. They had to slow down for a few bends but kept that pace until just before Graham, were Jack saw some sort of roadblock ahead. Ralph got on the CB and let the others know why they were stopping. It wasn't a heavy obstacle and their vehicles could probably blow right through. As far as Jack could tell, it was just a makeshift gate and the few men.

They couldn't tell if it was military, police, or worse. As they discussed whether to go around or go through, the people responsible for the roadblock opened fire.

Josh picked up the mike and said, "Let me take the lead, we've got a surprise for them!" He told John to get the goggles out of the glove box and put them on. Then he reached behind him and handed John a SAW and said, "Light them up!" Then he hit the gas and the others followed. The people riding shotgun in the other vehicles got a reminder of why that seat was called 'shotgun' and opened fire. They weren't needed, however, as the SAW scattered the men in an instant. A few of them got hit but nobody counted how many. After they crashed through, Josh turned once they reached 224th St. E. He decided the side roads would be safer to get through just in case they had another roadblock on the other side of town. Once they got out of Graham, they returned to the main road until they reached Puyallup.

Jack got on the radio and said, "What were they thinking? That was a harebrained idea to open fire on people you know nothing about. They're either starving or stupid. Maybe both. Josh, you keep the lead. We're close enough to Puyallup and you know exactly where we're going."

Josh said, "Good plan."

On the other side of Graham, they got back onto 161 for a few miles. In Puyallup, they hit the side roads again until they reached 132nd St. E. Then Josh turned back to 161, now called Meridian, and turned right to get to a shop. They passed the theater and Jack and old memories flooded Jack's mind. He told Ralph, "I've had more than a few dates in that theater."

Ralph said, "Yeah, me too. Remember the old Earthquake Burger? I loved that place."

Jack said, "Oh my God, those were grubbin burgers. And so freaking huge!"

As they were reminiscing, Josh got on the radio and said, "We're here. Park behind the store so nobody sees us. Our target is there too." They parked the vehicles and Jack grabbed a few shovels in the back of his truck and Josh took one out of his truck. Josh said, "Someone blasted the front door, did you see that? That was a reinforced door with a security door in front of it."

Jason said, "It was probably the military getting weapons before anyone else could. Who else could blow through that door? I mean, besides you and your C4."

"I am a man of many talents," Josh said.

The few who heard that before laughed. The others wondered what they had missed.

Jack said, "I need two on the roof for lookouts. Jason is one, who else?"

Jim, the Eatonville driver said, "I've got good eyes. I'll go."

Josh parked the Bronco deliberately to help them climb to the roof. The first three men started digging where Josh pointed, they would switch out as they got tired. Josh said, "Don't worry, we only have to go down 2 feet. But we have to dig 5 feet by about 2 1/2 feet to get the door open." With six men and three shovels, they were able to get the job done in a hurry. As they were nearing their goal, Jason spotted a young man or teenager approaching and not hiding the fact that he was looking at the gun shop. He looked up and saw Jason then started to turn around.

Jason said, "I don't think so, kid. Stop, turn around, and continue the direction you were going." He chambered a round to drive the point home. The young man froze for a few seconds and did as as Jason said. As he passed by the gun shop, it looked like he was holding his breath and waiting to die. After he passed, Jason walked to the back and said, "You guys need to hurry. That kid is going to turn as soon as he can and double back to tell whoever he was spotting for what he saw."

Josh said, "We only need a few more minutes. You should've held him here."

When Josh buried the safe, he covered the combination dial with a few layers of burlap and strong plastic. He used duct tape to hold it all down. The tape had been there so long that he needed his knife to scrape it off and get to the dial. Then he pulled the solar flashlight out of his bag and turned it on. "Well, that sucks." The light was too dim to see so he handed it to Jack and said, "Turn that hand crank and shine it on the dial, it should only take me a few seconds."

True to his word, he had the door open in about 15 seconds. Josh said, "Load up and let's get out of here." In the safe were two Claymore's, a box of grenades, one of the SAWs, one of the Barrett sniper rifles, 4 night vision goggles, various hand-guns, and some ammo. As they were loading up, Jack asked, "Why did you bury this here when you have the stash at home?"

Josh said, "I didn't want all my eggs in one basket. And I wanted something a little closer to work if I needed some backup. Mostly the latter."

Jack said, "Let's get outta here before trouble shows up. Lead the way, Josh."

They got back on Meridian and made an immediate right onto 128 St. East. Josh led them on a series of turns but made it to the house in about 10 minutes. He parked on the street and watched the house with his night vision goggles to be sure no one was moving around in there. When he felt comfortable, he rolled into the driveway and parked. Then he ran up and opened the gate to the back yard. He got back to his truck and drove behind the house. Then he backed up his truck on the far end of the lawn. Josh picked up the mic and told everyone else to back in as well. He told Jim to park the box truck next to him. He would be closest to the stash since he would be carrying most of it.

Mark said, "Why don't we just load everything in the box truck and make it easy."

Josh said, "Remember what I said earlier? Don't put all your eggs in one basket. If anything happens to the truck, we lose everything. Spread it out and we only lose whatever is in the truck we lost."

Mark said, "Okay. That sounds reasonable."

Josh unlocked and opened the fallout shelter. He turned on the first lantern and said, "Good news, the batteries are still good. These are coming with us." Then he turned on two more lanterns and lit the area well. "All right, gentlemen. Let's clear this place out." The loot here included the other Barrett sniper rifle, two more SAWs, more Claymore's and grenades, three footlockers full of AR-15's, some handguns, suppressors, flash bangs, the body armor, more night vision goggles, compound bows, lots of arrows and tips, and other archery equipment and supplies. There were also a few foot-lockers full of ammo, mostly for the AR 15's, but various other rounds as well. There were gunpowder and everything else for the reloading machine. Finally, he had ten buckets of mountain house pouches and several cases of emergency water for his personal stash.

As they were loading, Jim thought he saw movement in an upstairs window. He went to the front of the truck and put on his goggles. He saw two people watching them, then warned the others. He said, "We are not alone here. I saw two people in the window, only heads. If they're armed, they aren't pointing at us."

Jack said, "Grab your rifle and keep an eye on them while we finish. They're probably just curious and a little worried."

Everyone else finished loading the trucks, removing the lanterns last.

Getting Home

W<small>HEN EVERYONE WAS IN THEIR VEHICLES,</small> J<small>OSH ROLLED HIS</small> window down and yelled out, "You can stay in my house for now, we got what we came for and we're leaving." Then he drove off, leading the way. Josh took almost the same route back towards Meridian. He planned to make a turn just before Meridian, but there was a new roadblock on 128 Street East. This one was flimsier than the one in Graham, obviously put together at the last moment. There would be no hesitation this time, however. Josh would make a small route change and turn directly on Meridian. It would be too dangerous to make a turn on the side street right after the roadblock.

Josh told John, "It's go time! Light them up." He didn't bother getting on the radio because once they heard the gunfire, they would know what to do. John opened fire and hit two of them, the other scrambled while taking pot shots at the vehicles. The others fired shots as they were driving by to make sure the would-be thieves stayed down. Josh saw another roadblock up ahead but made a quick left into an apartment complex to avoid it. He had been through here several times while testing escape routes for Sam. So, he knew it would let them out on 132nd St. E. From there he weaved through the many back streets, always making his way toward Graham.

They felt relieved when they finally made their way out Puyallup and were able to get back on Meridian. As they neared Graham, Josh heard a lot of noise coming from the back of his truck. The truck was shaking and Josh said, "A flat tire, now?" He slowed down and pulled over, then John got on the radio and told everyone what was going on. They got out of their vehicles and Josh said, "Help me unload, I have a hydraulic jack to get this beast lifted. This spot isn't safe, so we need to expedite." They unloaded his truck, moving fast but had to be careful because he had the gunpowder.

Josh got his jack then removed his spare and started on the lug nuts. Then they lifted the truck and Jim, back to being lookout with Jason, said they were men approaching. Those who had night vision goggles donned them. Everyone grabbed their weapons and spread out. Jack could make out five bodies about 100 yards away and getting closer. At about 50 yards, Jack saw they were armed and yelled out, "That's far enough. Turn around."

One of the men said, "You are trespassing and need to pay the fine."

Jack said, "This is a public road and has already been paid for. Turn around."

The other man said, "Not anymore, it's our road now and you can either pay the fine or meet your end."

Jack said, "You can have it back when we leave. For now, you need to turn around and walk away. Each one of you is covered by a rifle. Walk away and live, or we will be forced to defend ourselves."

The men talked amongst themselves for about 30 seconds then turned around and walked away. They didn't say anything else to Jack. Just when Jack thought it was over the men spun and opened fire. None of the Graham men were wearing night vision goggles and none of them hit anything. John was ready and opened up with the saw. The men were walking close together and were cut down in a flash. The others fired as well, but there was no telling if they hit a target because the saw was so effective. When it was over John said, "Hey Josh, do you have any more ammo for this? I'm out." Josh said that was it and he would have to switch to his rifle.

Mark and John collected the weapons of the dead man while Josh finished changing the tire. Then they loaded the truck up again and continued their journey home. Once again, they all veered off to the side streets to get through Graham. As they neared the other side, they saw another roving patrol. There was no doubt they heard the gunfire from earlier, so Josh stopped his truck about 100 yards away and yelled, "Turn around and walk away. Your friends made the wrong choice, how will you choose?" These men were much smarter, it only took them a few seconds to come to the conclusion that they were outgunned. They did as told and walked away.

Jack was happy this one ended without violence. The experience made him happy they lived far away, and that he lived in an area where he and his friends could control the community. After Graham, they were back on 161 headed to Eatonville. The drive to Eatonville was so quiet, Jack felt he could go to sleep. They went from blood pumping adrenaline to silence. They radioed ahead to let Richard know they would be there soon. So, when they pulled into the gas station, Richard was ready for them. Everyone got out and filled their vehicles. Jack saw Calvin approaching and ask Ralph to take over the pump.

Calvin walked up and handed Jack a crate and said, "Two hens and a rooster. Now you'll have an easier time feeding those extra mouths, and you can start breeding more chickens."

Jack took the crate and said, "Your kindness knows no bounds. I thought you were too old to stay up late?"

Calvin said, "I said, I was too old to stay up late and lift heavy objects."

The two men laughed, and Jack put the crate in his truck. While Jack was back there, he grabbed two 9mm handguns and some ammo.

Jack said, "Your kindness cannot go unrewarded." He handed the weapons and ammo to Calvin and said, "Thank you, I mean it."

Calvin said, "One more thing. That sack over there is yours too, it's full of feed for the chickens. Make sure to grow some food for them in the spring."

Jack shook his head and said, "Once again, far too kind."

Jack retrieved the sack and squeezed it into the back of his truck. He thanked Richard for the fuel, and everyone said their goodbyes. The next stop was Elbe to drop John off. He was the only man in the group that would sleep in his own bed tonight. They made it there in good time and then continued on to the last leg of their trip. When they got to Ashford, Josh got on the radio and said, "We're close enough to Paul's that we can put the goggles away and switch to headlights, what do you think?"

Jason didn't waste any time and said, "No! Never assume you are safe. I did that and Brett died. We are never safe."

They kept the headlights off and made it to Paul's house. Jack was surprised Paul was waiting for him and said so.

Paul said, "I'd like you to be impressed, but I was sleeping until a few minutes ago. Sam manned the radio and let me know you were close."

Jack said, "All the same, you were still out here waiting for us."

Paul said, "I heard you had a few problems."

Jack said, "We did, and we'd be happy to tell you about them at breakfast. We are all pretty tired."

Paul said, "Of course, how silly of me. Come on in and get some well-deserved sleep. Larry and Tim will guard the vehicles until morning."

Everyone went inside, and Paul showed them to their beds. The next morning, they all shared a large breakfast of bacon, eggs, ham, cornbread, and coffee. Jack filled Paul in on the events, and the others added their comments as well. Paul said, "So what did we learn?"

Jack said, "Wear body armor on every mission."

Josh said, "Bring more ammo for the SAW."

Ralph said, "Bring a pair of clean underwear."

They all laughed at his joke and finished their breakfast.

After breakfast, they drove the vehicle to the warehouse and unloaded most of the contents into the warehouse. Josh kept one of the sniper rifles, a few rifles, handguns, and ammo for all of them. If Robin proves to be a competent sniper, she will take charge of the other sniper rifle. He also kept his meal pouches and water. For Eatonville, Paul gave them a SAW, some body armor, night vision goggles, a few AR-15's, and some ammo.

Jack said, "Thank you all for helping, it was much appreciated. I'd love to stay and chat, but I'd just like to get home and relax."

They said their goodbyes and Jack went home.

Final Preparations

PAUL STOOD OUTSIDE AND WAITED FOR HIS GUESTS TO arrive. Josh and Robin arrived a few hours ago for Robin's first lesson with him. Today they were still using an AR-15 for the training because she would not be taking any monster shots in the near future. Everything at Longmire was well within her range. Today he is only teaching her the basics and showing her some breathing exercises. First to arrive, as usual, were Jack and Diane. Paul greeted them and sent them inside.

They went in and saw Sam and Jason sitting on the couch. Sam stood and asked Robin how she was feeling. She said, "I'm feeling better now, thanks." She shook her head just enough for him to see she hadn't told Jack about the pregnancy yet. Then she said, "How is your family?"

Sam said, "They're good. Viktoriya, Kevin, and Mercy are watching Robin with her sniper training. Maybe one of them will step up soon. Larry and Martha will take them when the meeting starts, and they all have a barbecue with my wife. They get spoiled every time we have a meeting."

Diane said, "I'm sure they'll have fun."

Jack asked Jason how he was feeling, and he said, "I'm much better, thanks. My time in this house is over. Tonight, I will sleep in my own cabin, in my own bed. Being waited on was fun, but I don't recommend getting shot for the privilege."

Jack shook his head and said, "I have no plans of following your footsteps on that route. I prefer my body not perforated, thanks."

Sam said, "He was right all along. His wound wasn't too bad, but I kept him around to be safe. I had to be sure an infection didn't set in. He's good company too."

Jason gave him a sideways glance but didn't say anything.

Nikki walked in and was followed by John and his escort a few minutes later. Within the next ten minutes, the whole group had gathered. Robin was allowed in this meeting because she would be taking a role in the fight. Ralph and Brandon were invited, but Jack preferred someone was at the cottage. He would fill them in on the plans. Paul allowed a few minutes for people to say their hellos and catch up, then he began the meeting.

He said, "Thanks for everyone being here and making it on time, or early." He looked at Jack and nodded as that sentence ended. Then he continued, "I've been in contact with Morton and Eatonville. We won't see Morton until it's over, they'll arrive from the other side of the river to cover our blind spot and prevent escape. Eatonville will join us as we attack from the west. I need to be clear on this, do not shoot towards the river. I don't want any friendly fire. Also, do not go past the admin buildings. Any armed men beyond those buildings will be taken out by the Morton crew. We have the cabins, the National Park Inn, all the way to the ranger station, and everything in between. That's where most of the fighting will take place."

Mark said, "What about Morton's line of fire? Won't they risk hitting us?"

Paul said, "There's always a risk, but they will not be shooting towards us. We attack from the west and the north. Morton will be on the south side and firing to the northeast. If we stick to the plan, the risk of friendly fire is reduced to almost nothing. The only person who will be shooting towards the river is Josh. We trust he won't miss his target. He and Robin will be on the north side, but Robin will be concentrating her fire to the southeast. Things will get crazy so if you absolutely must fire towards the river, *don't miss*. Have I missed anything?"

Jack said, "The Friendlies in red hats. None of the women are armed, so don't shoot them. Do not shoot the children. Anyone wearing a red hat is an ally. Do not shoot them unless they're pointing a weapon at you. The red hat idea is not foolproof so be careful. All other armed men are fair targets."

Paul said, "Thanks Jack, that is an important point. Okay Doc, you're finally getting out of the house. You will hang back in a truck with Diane and John protecting you."

Sam said, "I'm a better shot than almost everyone in this room. I can handle myself and go with the rest of you, no offense to Diane and John."

Paul said, "I'm fully aware of your prowess with rifles and handguns. I'm also aware that you're the only doctor around and we can't lose you. If you get shot, who's going to fix you up? Do you want me fiddling around in your innards searching for bullet fragments? If any of them get past our line, you can take the first shot."

Sam nodded and gave up his quest to join in the action.

Josh said, "It would be nice if we had some live aerial surveillance. I have a drone, but my phone doesn't work."

Jack said, "I haven't thought about phones in months. My phone still works, as does Diane's. You can use mine."

Josh said, "I could if you had the software installed. It would be difficult to download it today."

"You forget I'm a software engineer. If you still have your phone, give it to me and I'll see if I can recover the software. If not, I can write something. But we would not have the drone for this fight. It would be useful later, however."

Paul said, "If nobody has anything else, I will see everyone here in two days.

John said, "I'll have my Rangers help. We left the park, but it's still our responsibility. We need to be a part of this."

"That would be great," Paul said. "We appreciate the help."

Winter War

EVERYONE WAS GATHERED AT PAUL'S HOUSE AND READY TO go. The Eatonville crew arrived the day before to be sure they arrived on time. The Morton crew would be in position by 4 PM. They had a longer, more difficult route and were on horseback. Everyone else would be driving. Paul went over the plan one more time while he had everyone in the same place. When he finished, he said, "Does anyone have any questions?" He waited a few moments, and nobody said anything, so he said, "Let's go!"

Jack kissed Diane and said, "Take good care of the doctor, I'll see you soon."

Diane said, "We'll be fine, you be careful and don't do anything stupid."

Jack got into his truck and waved goodbye to Diane.

Their sizable convoy left Paul's house and made their way to Longmire. They drove through the long-abandoned Nisqually entrance, and John remembered better times. He could see the booths with Rangers welcoming vehicles. Then they went away, and he remembered the makeshift gate they made and the long line of cars waiting to get in. He remembered Stewie riling everyone up and the Rangers giving up and letting everyone in. He wondered what happened to Stewie after he took him to jail. Was he still there? Did they let him out? John figured he would never know the answer and brought himself back to real time.

Jack only remembered meeting John at the entrance after Diane had shot and killed her would-be rapist. Then they met again, a little while later. They stopped about a mile from Longmire and piled out of their vehicles. They would walk the rest of the way in, so the engines didn't give them away. Diane, John, and Sam would wait here until they received the message to move forward. Those who had it, strapped on their body armor. Jack carried an AR-15 and his trusty Colt 9mm. He carried two magazines on his belt and put two more in his backpack with his night vision goggles, first-aid supplies, and a few other goodies. He wasn't sure he needed the goggles, but it was better to be prepared. If the fight lasted more than thirty minutes, he would need them.

Jason needed a new partner to scout with, and Jim from the Eatonville crew volunteered. He said, "I told you I have good eyes."

Jason said, "I remember, and I agree. Let's go."

The two scouts walked into the trees and made their way towards Longmire. The rest of the group waited five minutes and started their hike as well. That's about the time Jason spotted two men on bikes and was confused. The guard change is at 4 o'clock, the time they planned the attack to start. He looked at his watch and saw that he was on time, it was the guards that were off track. As they got closer, he pulled his sidearm and screwed on the suppressor. Then he noticed it looked like the same two men that shot him and Brett. That made what he was about to do a lot easier. Then he put a .45 round in each of their heads. The two scouts moved ahead and stripped the bodies of their weapons. Then they disappeared back into the woods and continued their way to Longmire. Jason got on the radio and let them know about the bodies they would discover soon. Then Jason and Jim made it to the roadblock and waited for the rest of the crew.

When they arrived, Josh took Robin, Jason, Jim, and two others to cover the north side. Josh and Robin would be sniping while the others protected them and take shots where they could. Josh stationed Robin just past the inn, and he moved forward to about the intersection. The rest of the group moved into the woods and spread out in a line moving towards the river. Nobody got close to the river, however. Their cue to move forward would be a shot fired by Jason. The group determined in advance that Jason would take the first shot, it seemed fitting. But now his first shot would be the third shot.

Jack got on the radio and asked JR Eaton, from the Morton crew, "Are you in position?" JR answered back, "Ready to rip."

Jack said, "It's time." Jason stood next to Robin and scanned the area and looked for a target. Next to the National Park Inn, Jason found what he was looking for. A large man with a rifle slung over his shoulder was walking toward the Ranger station. It was an easy shot, about 60 yards, and Jason took aim, let out a slow breath, and fired. The man fell. Then... silence. Nobody expected silence.

Time slowed down and the two minutes of nothing felt like

two hours. Then someone pushed a woman out of a building, but nobody took the bait. She ran to the inn and ducked inside. Within a minute, they noticed men darting between trees. Robin saw a man on the second floor of the inn. He had a rifle and was looking for a target. Robin took aim and squeezed the trigger with a gentle touch. The round ripped into the man's chest and he fell back. They heard shots firing from the south and knew Morton had engaged the enemy.

Jack motioned the line to move forward, and they took slow steps toward the cabins and inn.

☙❧

Sgt. Baker heard the shot and knew it was time. He grabbed his weapon and his hat and ran to Cpl. Isaacson's room. Isaacson had the same idea and they met in the hallway. Then they knocked on the doors of the men who were with them and told them what was going on. Baker made one more stop at Julie's room and told her and her son to hide under the bed. The lieutenant had a cabin, but Julie told him he should wear his red hat every day. When he asked why, she only said, "I like it and it will keep you safe. Promise me you'll wear it every day, no matter what." Then she remembered, he would still try to shoot intruders. She told her son to stay under the bed, and she would be back soon. Then she ran past Baker into the lieutenant's cabin.

Baker and the rest of the Red Hat crew went outside and hoped they wouldn't get shot. They made a beeline for the Ranger station, knowing the general would still be in there expecting everyone else to do the fighting. Robin saw the group of men with red hats and let them pass. Julie made it to the cabin and pounded on the door saying, "Let me in, Dan!"

The door opened just enough for Julie to squeeze through. She said, "Put on that hat and wait here. Do not shoot anybody. Don't even pick up a gun. The general is going down. As long as you keep the red hat on and don't shoot anyone, you'll be safe." Then she darted out the door and ran back to be with her son.

Jack's line moved closer and started picking off enemies as they moved. Josh saw a man in a red hat running towards the inn and let him go. The man moved around the end and saw Jack coming. He raised his rifle toward Jack and aimed, but fell dead before he could take a shot. Jack never saw the man. They moved closer still, with shots firing off all around. Jack took a round to the gut and fell to the ground. He thought he was going to die until he remembered he was wearing body armor. He looked down and the round had hit a plate. He said, "My lucky day." Then he got up thinking, *I'm too old for this*. He got on the radio and told JR, "We're moving towards the Ranger station. It's time for you to cross the bridge."

Sgt. Baker and his group made it to the general's office and slipped inside. They found the general cowering in the corner behind his desk and the colonel hiding behind his desk. Baker wanted to calm their fears, hoping they would get comfortable. What looked like cowering, could be hiding something. He said, "General, what are your orders?"

The general got up with the slow movements of an overweight man. His eyes darted around, but he avoided direct eye contact with anyone. He said, "Get out there and fight!" He saw the general was unarmed and asked the colonel to lead them. The colonel stood with a 9mm in his hand. As he walked towards the door, one of Baker's men yelled, It's a trap!"

Baker shot him in the head Pointblank. The colonel raised his weapon, but Isaacson was faster and put two rounds center mass. The colonel fell back into his desk and didn't move. The general went back to cowering in his corner. Baker forced him to stand and frisked him. Then he sat the general in his chair and made him face the corner. Baker checked the general's desk for weapons but didn't find any. He said, "You must have felt really comfortable in here."

A few minutes later the shooting died down. Baker opened the door enough to stick his hand out and wave the red hat around. Jack radioed Diane and told her to bring the doctor in. He sent six people to clear the inn, and moved toward the Ranger station. As he got close, he saw someone waving a red hat through the door. He got within a few yards of the Ranger station when he heard a shot from inside the inn. He debated running over to check it out but trusted his men and stayed the course.

He waved John and a few more men over to join him outside the Ranger station. He said, "Everybody come out unarmed and hands up."

Baker said, "I'm sending the general out first. Everyone else is with me."

The general walked out with his arms in the air, and Jack told him to get face down on the ground. Then the rest came out one by one. Jack asked, "What about the hunters, where are they?"

Baker said, "They're all here, I'm one of them. You picked a good day, nobody went out today. Two people left a little while ago to look for horses, did you see them?"

Jack said, "They were taken care of."

Baker said, "A few neighbors, eh?"

Jack walked over and looked down on the general and said, "Well, general. It's nice to finally meet you."

Interrogation

THE GENERAL SAID, "WHO ARE YOU?"

Jack said, "I'm a friend of the man your man shot and killed, on your orders. Maybe you know my friend Jason, he was shot too."

The general said, "I don't know what you're talking about. I didn't order anything."

The red hats chimed in and called him a liar. Pvt. Rafino came running up and also called him a liar and said, "I was there when you ordered it, right there in your office."

Jack saw he wasn't wearing a red hat and said, "Who are you?"

"I'm Joel Rafino. I took charge after the Rangers left, and these guys came in with their guns and started ordering everyone around."

The general said, "All of you would've been dead by now if we hadn't arrived. You're so incompetent you couldn't lead a kindergarten class around a track."

Rafino said, "We were all doing our part, then that guy moved everyone around and told a few of the women they weren't pulling their weight. Then he sent them to that building over there and made it a brothel. He told them they could work there, or they could leave, knowing if they left they would die. The women understood that choice as well."

Jack said, "You didn't make too many friends here did you gen... What's your name?"

The general said, "Ike Tindal."

"What service did you serve in?"

Ike said, "None. I was never in the military. The ranks made things easier."

Everyone had started gathering around, and Julie came to confront her tormentor. She said, "This oaf wanted me in that brothel too and everyone knew it. But first, he wanted me for himself. That was your mistake, old man. I helped set all this up because you were never going to lay a hand on me."

Jack said, "You have committed a lot of crimes, Ike Tindal. We don't have time for a fair trial, so I'll take the word of everyone around you. Jason, would you like the honors?"

Jason's response was to put around in Ike's head.

Jack took Baker aside and said he wouldn't mind if he lead Longmire from now on but said they could choose amongst themselves, as long as Joel is never in charge. Then he went to check with Sam about the wounded. Sam said, "We have three wounded but nothing serious. One died, it was one of John's Rangers."

Jack said, "We'll have to make sure to take care of his family."

He heard someone behind them say, "Hi sweetie, remember me?"

Jack remembered that voice and that tone and turned to see Chuck Whidden standing there with a goofy grin on his face. He said, "Hello Chuck, I see you haven't lost your touch."

JR said, "Lucky for you too, he saved your butt."

Jack scratched his eyebrows and said, "What do you mean?"

"Didn't I mention? Chuck is our sniper. We had Chuck high in a tree. Someone had a bead on you and Chuck took him out."

Jack said, "No, you only said he was good at comic relief." Jack looked at Chuck and nodded his head then said, "Thanks Chuck, I owe you one."

Charles pulled off his backpack and pulled out a 2-liter bottle of homebrew. He said, "Here sweetie, I made this just for you." And he gave an exaggerated wink and pursed his lips then said, "Give Chucky a big kiss."

Jack said, "I'll give you a handshake but don't get that mouth near me."

The three of them laughed and Jack said to JR, "Are you sure he's just joking?"

JR said, "Mostly sure."

Jack shook his head and transferred the beer to his backpack.

Sam saw a redhead walking around and recognized her. He said, "Hey! I know you."

The woman turned around and saw the doctor and recognition showed on her face. She said, "You're with them? How did you get here?"

Sam said, "I was about to ask you the same thing. You're a long way from the FEMA camp. And yes, I'm with them."

She told Sam how they left the camp and made their way to Ashford, where his friends killed her husband. And then her trip to the park. She said, "I know he shot first, but that doesn't take the sting away. I have mixed emotions about all this. They killed my husband, but they saved me from that monster. You helped me, but you're also with them. It's all so confusing, I need to work it out."

Sam said, "I'm sorry. I saw a lot of patients and don't remember your name."

"Julie, Julie Roberts."

Sam said, "It's nice to see you again Julie Roberts. I need to get back to my patients here, I'll talk to you later."

Julie said, "I'll see you later."

After Sam got the wounded patched up and ready to go, they put the men in the truck with a few guards and Sam drove them back to the vehicles. They waited there for everyone else to show up. Then everyone drove to Paul's for a debrief.

Debrief

THEY ALL PILED INTO PAUL'S LIVING ROOM FOR THE debrief. He said, "We will have to keep an eye on Longmire. We won't offer help at this time except to remain allies. This is just the beginning, it's only going to get worse when people start to migrate this far out. The suburbs are bad, all the way out to Graham. People will keep moving east to escape the danger. I think it's time we prepare for the convocation. We can start with Brandon and Ralph."

Brandon and Ralph looked around because they had no idea what the convocation was, and why it was starting with them. Paul noticed the looks and said, "Don't worry, I'm sure Jack will explain it to you." Then he continued, "Hunting in the park is back on, but I still don't want anyone out alone. Stick with two or more people as a rule. Robin, I'm told you did well, and Josh is looking forward to your continued training. We'd also like to invite you formally to join our group."

Robin said, "I'd be delighted, thank you."

Jack, Diane, Brandon, and Ralph got back to the cottage that night. Jack explained the convocation to all of them. He said, "The convocation is a big step and means none of this is going to end soon. It also means Paul thinks it really is going to get worse. We will be building cabins close together on Paul's property. We'll be one small community with a lot of firepower. We'll have farm fields and good company. It also means you two are moving again because you're getting the first cabin, but you're also building it. Paul is an excellent carpenter and will be helping. But don't fret, that won't happen until springtime. We aren't going to build in the winter."

Diane said, "Jack, I need to speak with you alone."

"Uh oh."

She said, "It's not bad, at least I don't think it is. Wait, are you feeling guilty about something?"

Jack denied guilt while walking to their bedroom. They entered the room and Diane shut the door and said, "Merry Christmas."

Jack looked at his watch and said, "Today is Christmas? I haven't paid attention to a calendar in weeks. I guess I didn't have time to do any shopping."

She said, "You already gave me the best gift I can have. As luck would have it, I'm giving you the same gift."

Jack furrowed his eyebrows but didn't say anything.

Diane took Jack's hands in hers and placed them on her belly and said, "Merry Christmas, daddy."

Want More?

WANT MORE

In this series:

Aftermath of Disaster: Book 1 It Has Begun

Aftermath of Disaster: Book 2 Diggin' In

Aftermath of Disaster: Book 3 Summer's End

Aftermath of Disaster: Books 1, 2, and 3 Bundle

Non-Fiction

How to Get off the Grid and Survive

Prepper Journal & Inventory Logbook

I'll keep you up to date

Sign up to get notified of my new releases

Visit my website to see all my books

https://kevinbarrymaguire.com

Thanks for purchasing this book, I hope you enjoyed it. I'd appreciate a review on Amazon. It really helps authors and I read them all. This series went from short stories to novel because the reviews kept saying "too short."

Thanks again,

Kevin